AGNES KAY-E

D1824200

Rhythm of the Wild Drum

&

Other Stories

Ebook ISBN 9789789523207
Paperback ISBN 9789789523214
Hardback ISBN 9789789523221

Illustrations by Chimele Ezinwo
Cover Photography from Chimele Ezinwo

God Almighty

Contents

Rhythm of the Wild Drum

- Prequel to Subservience

Before recorded history, there was a land of twelve kingdoms called Evóvuotu. It was so-called because it

consisted of two kinds of people: the Okoruchi, and the Ehuehu. They were ruled by the King of All Living Folks. While there was a King of all living folks, there was also a Chieftain of Divinity, Wealth & Duty.

Rhythm of the Wild Drum & Other Stories

The Chieftain of Divinity, Wealth & Duty was gifted with Anya'ogu and was the keeper of Ófòr-Oguneli. His supreme duty was to ensure there was no breach of duty by the Okoruchis and to guide the Paramount Ruler. He was also to counsel the king as well as ordain one when it was required. Paramount Rulers, although of equal ranking as the Lord Marshals, never joined the army but had similar training as everyone born in Evóvuotu.

However, the Chieftain of Divinity, Wealth & Duty was usually born on a day without the sun, rain, or a cloud in the sky. It was an unusual occurrence as the birthday had to be in between two rainy days before the harvest season began. If there was no Chieftain, then the King of all folks took on the responsibility of the Ófòr-Oguneli for safekeeping until one was available.

1.

Several seasons had passed since Anyanwuze, offspring of Egbe became the King of all Living Folks. He became caretaker of the Ófòr-Oguneli handed him by his de'nnâ. As the caretaker, he had a vague ability to wield its powers. However, the powers not being his to wield drained him of his physical element, thereby depleting his lifespan (a precaution and a deterrent).

It was the first time since the reunion of the twelve Kingdoms that it had no chieftain since the early passing of the last one during the reign of Egbe, de'nnâ of Anyanwuze. The last of the Paramount Rulers had passed away eighty cycles ago, sixty cycles after the last Chieftain. As none of them had handed their totem capes to their kin, their powers automatically returned to Ófòr-Oguneli. (Anyanwuze was a prince but not made crown prince at the time because he was still a childling when the last chieftain died.) Fortunately, the Paramount rulers lived long and were borderline corrupt.

Anyanwuze, offspring of Egbe and King of all Living Folks was an old merfolk saddled with choosing his successor. His favourite and most capable offspring was taken from him to the great beyond, but destiny had fortunately left him five offshoots. He adopted his late nwónnenanna's offspring, but as they came of age, they grew greedy and hostile. Three of these offshoots got his attention, but he waited to see the one that'll develop the spirit of kindness. He set tests for them, and they continually failed until he gave up. One of them was Uzò. King Anyanwuze had three refrains for his offspring's offshoot: a leader does not cower or hide when bullied or threatened; shouldn't be generous to his enemies; and, must seek to enrich his Kingdom.

3

With time Uzò, (nicknamed Okpararebisi because he liked to be in charge of the food) caught his attention and quickly became his favourite. Uzò a.k.a. Okpararebisi was the youngest of King Anyanwuze's offshoots, a carbon copy of his de'nnâ, he was kind and generous, but the King suspected he would make a weak leader and couldn't run the affairs of his compound much less a kingdom.

Okpararebisi was now king. During his reign, there were no Paramount Rulers because a Chieftain of Divinity, Wealth & Duty had not yet been born. Okpararebisi reigned without interference, but he was nearing his end, and no hope was in sight. With all the powers he took from the Ófòr-Oguneli, he could not cause his wives to birth him an heir to the throne. Desperate, he searched far and wide for an antidote to extend his life span or a legitimate offspring to carry on his legacy. He had used every lore he could evoke from the powers in the Ófòr-Oguneli all to no avail.

Okpararebisi was now a Master of Illusion so much so that he looked young, lean, and agile to everyone who came across him though he was the exact opposite. But when the date has been fixed in someone's timeline, only the Lord of All could extend it, and everyone knew that immortality was a tale by moonlight to teach childlings morals.

The Ófòr-Oguneli would have to be handed over to a new King. It was too much power for a simple folk, yet no babelings were born on the said day in the twelve Kingdoms. At least that was what all living folks believed, but Okpararebisi knew better. He always knew, for the Ófòr-Oguneli's true glory shone, then he'd trace the babeling and murder it. But unbeknownst to him, not far away from the palace Kingdom of El'ikenueze, just below the borders of the northern Kingdom of Rumuochara, a place designated for the unusual, the cruel, the atrocious, and even the lewd, a

4

babeling was born.

Meanwhile, Nkóli, the queen of Rimeóku, the weemate of Okwelewe, King of Rimeóku was missing.

The first time she'd escaped was during the reign of Anyanwuze's de'nnâ, and he let it slide because he could see

her – it came from being mated. Okwelewe understood her loneliness; Rimeòku was a desolate realm for a living folk -

5

nothing grew, nothing lived. He let her get a taste of her old realm if only to stop her from turning spiteful.

This time he couldn't feel, sense, or find her. He had a feeling that one of his nwónnenanna may have helped hide her. He didn't know of any other power strong enough to obscure his sight. Whoever or whatever it was gave him a cause for concern. He decided to visit the world of living folks. It was the only place she had ever visited, the only realm she'd ever known, so he thought it wise to start there. He would have readily gotten rid of her, but his de'nnâ had permitted him only one weefolk, leaving him no choice but to find Nkóli and bring her back.

Okwelewe, the King of all Dead Folks didn't know what love was, but he knew immortality was torture without a companion and he knew the stirrings of the loin had to be gratified.

Out of semi-genuine concern for his weemate, Okwelewe left the affairs of Rimeóku to his first offspring Ónwu and went off in search of Nkóli. He refused to hand his sceptre to Ónwu because of his careless curiosity and knew it would be a slight on Ónwu if he handed it to any of his younger nwónnenanna. He couldn't take it with him to the realm of living folks because Nkeazu, the keeper of the barrier between realms, would rather die than let it pass through her woods. Besides, if he left with it, the Lord of All would discover that he left his post. A forbidden act.

Ónwu, the soul reaper was bored with handling his de'nnâ's mundane duties even though he enjoyed it, its repetitiveness was driving him insane. He wanted something more, approximately new and possibly intriguing. His de'nnâ was supposed to have been back ten cycles ago.

One day he wandered into his de'nnâ's throne-room and picked up his de'nnâ's sceptre and caressed it like he always

6

did. As he did, he felt a sensation from the tip of his fingers work its way up to the rest of his body. He started to scream from the pain and then from the fright of being transformed. He tried to shake off his de'nnâ's sceptre, but it was stuck to his hand.

Not long after he could hear his nwónnenanna, Kagbuo and Nonw'elizie screaming then passed out. When they came through, they were different, in the land of living folks they would be called grotesque.

Ónwu's jaw elongated, his eyes were as red as blood and his brows wispy white, his complexion as dark as night, his pets turned into the likeness of goats with elongated jaws, fanglike goatee, their hinds long and thin with spikes on the head and eyes to match his.

His buxom Nwónnenanna, Nonw'elizie was now thin, without eyes and looked like a ghost. One half of Kagbuo's body was living folk worthy with a wispy blackness in place of an eye, and the other half was bones; his skeletal half had orbish-eyes in its socket. He had a gnarled bone around his waist. They all had a ghostly trim from their waist down.

"What have you done?" Kagbuo asked, angrily.

Before Ónwu could answer, he was whisked to the balcony of the palace. Beside it, a chariot began to form from rising bones sewn together of their own accord. As soon as it was completed, his gnarly, goatlike pets rose to it and huskily neighed. He caressed his pets and giggled, but it sounded like a thin cackle. Kagbuo covered the ear of the living side of his body.

Ónwu squinted and tilted his head. Ideas filled his thoughts, and he formed a desire, a desire to visit the realm of living folks. A realm that could keep his de'nnâ from returning to his duties was a realm worthy of his visit. The problem was that he couldn't go through the portal unless his de'nnâ consented. One day he discovered that it was easy to leave when a soul had reached atonement status. Outside the realm of Rimeóku was the Enwere tree folks of the realm between realms and Nkeazu, the leadtrunk, wouldn't let him pass.

After too many failed attempts, he befriended Icherekini, Nkeazu's offspring. In one of their negotiations, he

discovered that the young Enwere were falling ill and a stench of rot oozed from them, but they wouldn't die. He made her swear an oath: if he succeeded in solving their problem, they would let him pass to the realm on the opposite side, and she agreed. His investigation revealed that they missed their family, a feeling that they were no longer supposed to have after their transition.

It wasn't hard for him to scoop water from the river of dead thoughts because Nonw'elizie, its guard, had strong stirrings for Icherekini. He poured droplets on the stumps of the young Enwere, the following day the realm smelt of wood and frost. It took three moons for Icherekini to repay his kindness.

Finally, free to roam the realm of living folks, he went through with the sceptre, but it returned to its cradle as soon as he set foot in Evóvuotu. He roamed for a season until he was bored. Time moved differently from his realm. Here, he didn't have a physical form so all they saw was an apparition at night and he enjoyed the fright he gave even if it was fleeting. He also noticed that he could permeate through anything, even people, and he could desire to be someplace else, and he would materialise there, albeit without form.

One day, he became curious of the couple who seemed so animated by laying atop each other and disturbing the otherwise rhythmic sound of the night. So, as the merfolk arched his back, he looked straight at the merfolk. The merfolk froze and then slumped. Instantly, an apparition, an exact replica of the merfolk escaped from the slumped body like a wisp of air. It lingered aimlessly and then came toward him. Startled, he shielded his face, but a light escaped from his wrist. He didn't remember wearing a wristband, but there was one on his wrist. It bore the symbol of his de'nnâ's authority. He turned his palm up, and the wristband expanded. After swallowing the apparition, the wristband returned to its former size just as the light disappeared.

Amused, Ónwu decided to find out how the wristband worked. He looked back at the weefolk as she struggled to get the dead merfolk off her, gasping and covering her mouth. She looked around as she pulled down her hide before running away. He laughed, and it sounded like a very bad laugh. Just then, his pets materialised before him, and he knew what to do.

A pungent smell wafted by. As soon as he caught the scent, he'd unintentionally materialise there. It didn't take him long to realise the odour was the stench of death. He also realised that he could now feel strange things in his body, which wasn't as translucent and bright as when he first entered the realm of living folks. It was curious and intriguing and somewhat scary, but it beat returning home. More so, this realm had colour, and he loved colour, especially the one that seeped out of the neck of a merfolk just before he got the apparition.

What he didn't realise was that as he lingered, several living folks fell ill with unidentifiable ailments. His pets lingered too, swallowing white goats so much so that goat owners started painting their goats, so the unknown thief would miss theirs.

Trying to catch an insect to halt boredom, he caught the stench of death and followed it. Confused at not finding an apparition, he began to suspect that the wristband was no longer working. The problem was that the stench was on a living folk. Intrigued, he waited, desiring the soul of this folk, so much so that he refused to follow any other apparition. That desire bound Ónwu to the realm of living folks like bees are bound to honey.

2.

Back in El'ikenueze, Okpararebisi toyed with the illusion of Chinasa he'd created. The maid sat in front of him in the final pose he'd chosen for her. But the illusion magnified his discontent and impatience and most of all, his desire for revenge. He had decided to move on by getting one of the weefolks he'd inherited from his de'nnâ's cousins to conceive. None did which only increased his anger and the guilt he felt for not waiting for his Chinasa. No living folk was innocent of his wrath. When the guilt wore off, he'd go back to deflowering the younglings of the palace kingdom. He took advantage of every weefolk he came across, not caring that they had a mate.

Now the twelve Kingdoms were really desperate for change since there were no blessings done before the planting season, the harvest had dwindled. There was a widespread drought, the streams and rivers had dried up in some Kingdoms, and the people have had to migrate. Some adversely affected went to other Kingdoms to work for food, some sold their younglings as slaves or gave their younglings off as wives for food. It was even rumoured that some lent their wives out to wanton merfolks.

An Elder from each household in Evóvuotu came to visit the King for counsel. It was the first time in recorded and unrecorded history that a meeting of that magnitude was taking place. It would have been a festival had it not been for the gloom that heralded the meeting. Restlessly, they waited for the appearance of their King.

One of those elders was Ónu from Rumuoriji, the southwest part of the palace Kingdom just beyond Njigi hills. He kissed his teeth several times as he waited. He was the only patient person in the group. Patient because he had something the twelve Kingdoms desired. He, however, hoped they were desperate enough to take in the news with open arms.

Soon after the King joined the meeting, they begun to discuss politics and tax. Ónu suggested; that the King in his infinite wisdom should hand the throne over to his cousin while they continued their search for the new Chieftain of Divinity, Wealth & Duty.

Okpararebisi raised a brow while he listened and pondered. He wanted to discharge them so he could rest his frail bones but needed to find out what the slippery folk called Ónu knew. After a while, he asked them to go home and ponder on Ónu's suggestion because he had a more pertinent concern; the next chieftain. For some reason, he couldn't find the Okoruchi that made the Ófòr-Oguneli glow just like he couldn't find a cure for his old age. It was a matter of time, He nodded and smiled to himself, he'd been getting rid of threats and traitors for so long he'd lost count. He had his cousin wrapped around his finger. He would never relinquish the throne to someone so gullible even it was his offspring.

The following day they reconvened at the palace. Soon after they cleared their itinerary Ónu stood up, clearing his throat.

"I have news," he said, kissing his teeth dramatically.

They responded with murmurs, some impatient, some sceptical but all eager.

"Because you are called Ónu does not necessarily mean you should use your mouth like a weefolk all the time," Omena'ala muttered in his raspy voice.

A few people lowered their head to laugh as it would have been an insult because Ónu was much older than them.

Ónu eyed Omena'ala of the palace Kingdom. They had been head-locked since Ahu gave Omena'ala the piece of land near the river beside El'ikenueze after he'd pledged it to him. "There is a childling born on the said day."

The news was followed by an excited buzz.

Ónu gestured for them to calm down before clearing his throat.

Okpararebisi raised his brows slightly, his interest piqued. He hadn't seen or felt the lull of the call, but he knew it was only a matter of time before the gods would try something new. However, hope was a risky business.

"Why are we hearing of this now?" Ômadike of Rumuochara asked, eyeing Ónu suspiciously.

"Where is this childling?" Someone in the back asked.

"Are you reeling us into one of your duplicitous schemes again?" asked Njuru of Eliotu, a former palace guard in the time of King Anyanwuze.

"Are you sure?" Mekaweli of the palace Kingdom inquired curiously.

Ónu rubbed his eyes to hide his grimace. This was why he hated these meetings. People always interrupted.

Okpararebisi was interested in this new development. As King, he was privy to information from all kinds of people, but this childling was unheard of and therefore an emergency problem. "Let him speak," he said softly turning his gaze to Ónu and urged him to continue.

"The childling is in the outskirts of this very village near the boundaries of Onyenwe." Ónu paused emphatically.

"How can? How come?" Nchi of Ochezo in Elichei Kingdom gasped.

Ome'e of Eli-Avali, the oldest of all the elders, took some snuff to his nose and sneezed before nodding. "I suspect it's Isekó."

"Eh?" Omena'ala gasped, his eye twitching. "Isekó!"

"Isekó? Of all places?" A young elder from Akpunwó of Eli-Avali asked.

Ónu ignored the young merfolk sitting next to him and

continued, "Born to Eriri."

"Which Eriri?"

"How many Eriris do you know?" Igala of Omeoha in Eliruzógu snapped at his friend.

"The murderer?" The youngest of the elders leapt up like something hot had been placed on his seat. "A leopard does not change its spots."

Everyone glared at him; he had used the wrong parable it seemed.

"Can a lion birth a snake?" Njinji of Elindichie asked, a little puzzled as he tapped on his walking stick.

"No o!" The elders chorused and began to whisper between themselves.

"But a childling is innocent of its de'nnâ's sins," Oche-Eze, the Chief Priest quietly added, rubbing his tired painted eye.

Ónu couldn't help but notice that the King was now in a pensive mood as the murmuring increased.

Okpararebisi raised a solitary finger, and everyone quieted then he gestured and the murmuring, though hushed, continued.

Amadi of Óròdomanya in Rumuije leaned further into his cane; his back was already hunched with age. He harrumphed several times to get the attention of the other elders then snapped. "What is the point of cutting off ringworm from a leprosy infested body? We need a Chieftain."

Fear gripped most of the elders, and while some averted their gazes, others looked questioningly at the King.

"No offence, Your Majesty, but you aren't getting any younger," Amadi of Óròdomanya finished with an exhausted sigh.

Okpararebisi nodded slowly. He'd learned long ago not to argue with Amadi. He was the most free-spoken person and the most respected he knew.

Onwuchekwa of Anyadike in Elidikenónu groaned, "Yes, of course, and if this childling was born on the said day that is all that matters."

"I think there is more," Omena'ala added when he saw Ónu still standing.

"You have all forgotten so easily how he beheaded his weemate because she helped his nwónna..." Igala spat in a strangled voice as he tried to be heard.

"Into his bed," Another elder muttered, and the others broke into laughter.

"I would have done the same thing," Ónu said matter-of-factly. Some of those laughing covered their mouths to hide the sound. "But that is not the issue."

"Then what is the issue? Because you do not farm does not mean -" Oongu of Eliotu stopped to soothe his shin.

Omerò had struck Oongu's shin with his cane and glared at him sternly and warned with a raised brow. "Sit down. He who has no head has no need for the cap."

Oongu glared back but did as he was told.

Igala smiled with kind eyes. "Wait until you are old enough, dear youngling. You're still new to these things."

Okpararebisi's patience was wearing thin. He needed to quench their thirst for his replacement as soon as possible. The meeting was getting rather long, and it was getting in the way of his thoughts.

Omena'ala grimaced and shook his head exasperatedly. "He just wants to waste our time as usual."

Incensed, Omerò asked. "What is the issue?"

Ónu paused dramatically and then casually said, "It is a girl childling."

3.

The assembly fell silent. Even the morning birds and the noisy turkeys that prided their nuisance in the palace seemed to have discovered silence. It was the first time they had been in that kind of dilemma. The elders, the chiefs, Paramount Rulers, and Lord Marshals, even the subjugates to the Paramount Rulers were all male. The only known female with the same quality of authority ever known was The White Priestess and the Queen. No merfolk sought the Queen's audience. The White Priestess was allowed the privilege of male audience's supplication if her husband became the go-between.

What would become of them should a weefolk become the Chieftain? Or worse still, if the Lord of All decided to make her the head of all living folks, a Queen?

This is going to be easier than I'd thought. Okpararebisi smiled inwardly. Knowing the ego of merfolk, he could get them to approve his offspring albeit illegitimate, who by all count was now a merfolk, and had excel in all rites of passage. He decided to wait until nightfall to meet with his offspring. He'd only known about his offspring when he was under Uzò's spell and hadn't seen him since. If they would not have his offspring as heir to the throne, then they should be better off without the Ófòr-Oguneli.

Okpararebisi grimaced. He still desired to have a babeling by a weefolk of his choosing, not Uzò. His stay with her, under her spell, was still sketchy and he'd rather be aware when he gives a weefolk the seed of his loins. He could sense the soul reaper close by, desperate as always. He'd begun to sense him a few seasons ago and still hadn't figured out how the reaper got out of Rimeóku.

However, how he got here was irrelevant, his concern was that hope had been rekindled, and he didn't have much time to snuff it out. He looked up, rising, and everyone else joined him. Sighing, he swept his eyes around one last time. Who knew what the future had in store for them should his offspring be King, but that was the only way he was going to relinquish the throne and perhaps Ófòr-Oguneli.

"Ónu, Omena'ala," he called and then whispered to one of the guards beside him and waited until the guard returned with four warriors and continued. "No merfolk will cut off his nose to spite his face."

The congregation nodded.

Okpararebisi reached out to the Ófòr-Oguneli but stopped himself long enough to reach Ófòr-Nkigwe. He raised the Ófòr-Nkigwe above his head and declared. "Our warriors will go with you to fetch the new Chieftain. This is

a time of change, after all. We must embrace it. Go and bring our babeling home."

"You are wise, your Majesty," Oche-Eze muttered with a curt nod. "It's only a merfolk that is blind and deaf that the elephant will trample upon." Oche-Eze was glad that they were coming to a consensus so he could go and investigate the rumours about his weemate as the gods had promised to grant him insight. He unfolded his legs in readiness to get up using his Ófòr as a prop when it began to vibrate. He immediately let go. Carrying his satchel, he moved towards the King and his counsel just as he started his incantations then he sat down folding his legs. He eulogised the ancestors of the twelve Kingdoms as he produced the tools of his trade.

Okpararebisi frowned, not liking where this was leading and unable to stop it.

Oche-Eze spread out a stripy animal skin and tossed his cowries onto it. He pondered for a while, shook his head, and tried again. He let out an exasperated sigh and scratched his bald head impatiently and tried again.

Everyone preened their eyes, some cleaned their ears. It was unusual for a divination during a large congregation unless it had been the reason for their convening.

Oche-Eze opened his raffia bag and produced two calabashes, one with murky liquid and the other with white powder. He cupped powder in his hand then opened his palm to blow the powder in four cardinal points. He lapped some of the murky liquid and did the same thing. He sighed dramatically, then dug the cowries out of his bag and tossed them lightly as he did more incantations. Finally, Oche-Eze slunk back from the cowries and looked again. He shook his head and shrugged forcefully. Shaking his head, he took another look and sighed dolefully.

The people began to murmur.

"Hear, hear!" Oche-Eze called out dutifully. "It happened in the dark, but the sun snuck in to expose its buttocks. Ah! The buttocks of a merfolk! Regality is in his scrotum? The wild drum he summoned by stroking its

18

slumber has a tune. The rhythm that was put to slumber before time has begun, the dreaded music of the formidable is beckoning to its drummer. The drum has recognised the one who stroked it and has demanded a dance. The time has come for it." He gathered his cowries still shaking his head dolefully. He picked his feather and used it to scribble on the ground, poured libations, eulogised the deities of the Evóvuotu, gathered the tools of his trade, got up and backed away from the King and his counsel until he reached his Ófòr.

There was a long pause. Everyone was expecting more information and perhaps a solution. The gods seemed to enjoy showing off their wisdom because the people were dazed with confusion.

"Is that all?" asked Omeneri of Imidike in Elidikenónu who had been quiet the whole time.

Oche-Eze peered at him, irritated. "I say what the gods lent my eyes to."

Omeneri was sure that there was more. "But-"

Oche-eze stared at him coolly, gritting his teeth. "The gods have spoken."

The elders chorused. "So be it."

Okpararebisi nodded and walked away from the meeting. The elders waited a few more minutes for him to disperse them with blessings or invite them for refreshments as was customary, but when he didn't they left for their homes, each lost in his own thoughts.

In the excitement, Ónu told his second weemate that the offspring of her Nwónnenanna would be crowned the next Chieftain. She was so excited that she dared to ask him to give her the whole details of the meeting. He was so glad that he would be affiliated with people of influence that he told her everything. She was quiet while he ate. He had just finished his last morsel of pounded yam before he realised that she hadn't told him how her day went. He frowned at her. She was supposed to be dancing and rejoicing. Eriri's offspring was after all her niece, but she was frowning.

He cleared his throat.

She didn't respond.

He washed his hands and wiped them on his goat-skin kilt before tilting her chin up to face him. "What is it?"

"My lord, the night has ears," She answered in a small voice.

"Speak to your husband," he commanded.

She fidgeted and exhaled deeply. "My lord, this is good news."

"But...?"

She laid her hands on his lap. "A mouse that removes the palm nut that turns out to be the bait of a trap should have known that palm nuts do not grow on the ground."

Ónu shook his head and kissed his teeth. "Thank you for the food."

Sensing his annoyance, she gathered the food bowls and quickly left for her food hut.

Ónu sighed reprimanding himself, his weemate's warnings had never failed him. He pondered, remembering the King's countenance towards the end of the meeting. *Four warriors! I was concerned about that. The King's*

20

willingness may indeed be a trap. I must leave at once! Quickly, Ónu summoned his weemate.

"Bring me my satchel."

He carried in his satchel gifts and a small a large flint in case the path his de'nnâ had once shown him was now overgrown, there had been a drought for so long the leaves had fallen off most of the trees not to talk of tall grasses. Following that path, he'll arrive at Isekó in a quarter-of-a-moon. He had to make sure to go unseen, so instead of lighting a torch, he caught as many fireflies as he could and put them in the gourd-lanthorn his offspring invented. Whatever his offspring had put inside, it made them stay. He felt a little guilty using the gourd-lanthorn - he didn't want a yellow-bellied offspring, but the devices he made always worked. He only began to appreciate it when people came to trade for it making his second weemate a wealthy weefolk.

4.

It wasn't quite dark, yet the moon shone. He got to Isekó when the moon was at its peak. He was so exhausted it was an effort to clap his hand (clapping was a way of announcing one's presence).

"Kpom, kpom, kpom, it is your favourite in-law o." Ónu called and clapped a few more times, but no one answered. He looked around; there were too many huts too close together. He felt claustrophobic staring at them. He knocked again, shuddering every time a cold wind passed over him and nearly died of fright when he felt a hand on his shoulder.

"Sorry, but there has been a lot of restlessness in the area," Eriri whispered and beckoned him to follow. They walked around the back of the hut and followed a narrow path until they came to the edge of the village, then they made a detour towards the stream when they heard a scream and rapid footsteps.

"Yey!" Ónu squeaked and stopped walking then turned around abruptly when he heard a shrill voice in the almost quiet night.

Eriri looked surreptitiously.

"Head-hunters?" Ónu asked as he attempted to cover his beefy neck with shaky hands. He was shaking so much that he may have been oblivious to the fact that he'd peed on himself.

Eriri raised a brow with a grimace as he eyed the burly merfolk's apprehensive state. "Be a merfolk!"

Ónu remained rooted to the spot as Eriri left the path. Eriri had to pull him out of the path and into a patch of dense thickets. It was difficult to see through them. Eriri no longer felt like hiding when he noticed that the caterwauls of the denizens were getting closer to his main hut. He got up, pulling the reluctant Ónu with him.

When Eriri got to the side of the hut, he found three badly mutilated bodies. He walked over to one, a weefolk, and knelt beside her, saying a word of prayer before gently shutting her staring eyes. "This is not the work of head-hunters." He muttered and rested his hands on his lap. He curiously frowned at the mutilated body of a merfolk with a clenched fist and struggled to open it. He took the piece of cloth out of the merfolk's hand. He got up slowly, sighing heavily.

"Why?" Eriri asked through clenched jaws as he got up.

Seeing the deformed bodies in the moonlight, Ónu's legs could no longer carry him, so he sat on a heap of soil in the corner of a cooking tent, biting his nails as his legs shook involuntarily.

"Why?" Eriri asked again, his back no longer turned to

Ónu, now livid. No one was supposed to know his offspring's natal day. But his ambitious relation had no virtue.

Ónu's eyes stayed fixed on the dead bodies.

"You gave me your word, you scoundrel."

"Hmm?" Ónu looked up, surprised, his thought still on the dead bodies.

"What did you think Uzò would do? Pat you on the back and give you half of the Kingdom?"

Ónu tried to blink the image away, but it wouldn't disappear. "Eh? It can't..."

Eriri glared at him.

Ónu held his mouth with his fingers and looked away.

"Ómalichanwa," Eriri called in a loud whisper, almost choking from fear. He removed the mat that covered the dugout.

"Mpa! Mpa, is that you?" She cried, crawling up from the ground.

Eriri sighed. Relieved tears dropped from his eyes as he hugged his offspring. He was glad for the hiding place.

"What if it wasn't me?" he asked.

"Who else knows my name?" she nudged him and peered over him. "Uncle!" she exclaimed as she jumped excitedly on Ónu.

Eriri couldn't blame her. Ónu was the only relative who visited, who knew of her existence, until now. He looked at her with concern. He needed to get her out of Isekó before daybreak. The planting season had ended a while ago. They would soon be in the middle of the harvesting season, and by his calculations, Ófòr-Oguneli would seek her in a few moons, on her sixteenth cycle. Its present owner will follow its scent. He was glad to have had the bunker installed and believed her nné's spirit protected her, but she needed more than a spirit protecting her. In the meantime, where was she safest? The farther away she was from the Ófòr-Oguneli, the better.

"Mpa?" Ómalichanwa tapped her de'nnâ on his shoulder.

Eriri raised a brow.

"You have been very quiet. Uncle is not himself.

Besides..." She looked back at her uncle before whispering into her de'nnâ's ear. "Ófòr-Oguneli has located me."

Eriri gasped. *It was early. Too early*.

"Mpa! More merfolks are coming, more than before."

"Go and get what you need. We must leave now!" Eriri said and quickly unsheathed his flinchete.

Ómalichanwa went to the hideout in the ground and pulled a string up like taking water out from a well. It brought up three sack bags.

"Óma-"

"Mpa!" Ómalichanwa whispered loudly, rubbing her ear and pointing outside. She froze briefly, her eyes blank then she quickly pulled her de'nnâ towards her uncle and held her breath. He didn't like the idea of waiting, especially as he hadn't found a safe distance between his offspring and the approaching invaders. He raised his flinchete all the same. Ómalichanwa placed a reassuring arm on her de'nnâ's shoulder then closed her eyes, tapping into the air around them and created an illusion.

A few seconds later, four warriors hurried in with flinchete raised; One of them fell into the bunker and broke his neck. Another looked in their direction, squinted, shrugged and left. The last two left after they'd scattered everything.

"Let's go!" Ómalichanwa said, heaving one of the bags onto her shoulder.

Ónu was still in a state of shock.

Eriri wanted to wake him up with a punch, but Ómalichanwa placed her hand on her de'nnâ's hand then he rewarded her with an unpleasant smile to which she playfully shook her head. Eriri grimaced as he watched his offspring; like her nné, she was patient, strong-willed, and kind.

She would listen, gesture, and nod. But listening to

something or someone? It was a new thing to him and now very frequent that he dreaded his inability to be prepared to take care of her.

They walked for a few miles through the densely covered Ahia forest, then came into a large expanse of farmland. She plucked a cocoyam leaf, marked it and turned it upside down for a few seconds then picked it up and fanned the air

in the direction of each cardinal point to find the direction of the wind. They felt the wind, but she couldn't make out its direction, so she tried again, and this time on their right, the wind pressed against their bodies from the side of the setting sun. She stopped fanning, and the breeze stopped.

She did it again, the wind pressed them from the side of the rising sun towards the side of the setting sun. She walked towards the side of the setting sun and disappeared.

Startled, Eriri milled around. There was nothing but the farmland. He let go of Ónu whom he had been dragging along and scratched his head, wondering how he was going to find her.

Ómalichanwa reappeared, frowning.

Eriri stumbled backwards.

"Mpa, come quickly *nawh*!" she murmured and vanished again.

Eriri hesitated. He stood close to where she disappeared and stretched out his hand. The whole of his arm was gone. He retrieved it, his heart pumping hard. He shoved Ónu in and Ónu disappeared. He rubbed his jaw and tried to process what he'd just seen when just her head appeared. He was so taken aback that he stumbled over a few moulds of loamy soil.

Ómalichanwa's worried face looked angry. "Mpa, don't forget the leaf."

Seeing just her head had unsettled him. He rejected his fears, sighed, and picked the leaf up. Before he could get a chance to change his mind, he held his breath and ran through the portal, tripped over Ónu and landed flat on his stomach. They had appeared on the path that smelt much worse than an animal farm. The iroko tree ahead of them made him realise that they were behind Ónu's compound. Eriri was impressed. This was what he needed to take his offspring out of danger. He'd allow her rest for the night and take her away from the palace Kingdom before the early birds came out for their worms.

"We must leave," Ónu was muttering more to himself than either of them.

"But you're going the wrong way." Eriri retorted,

27

irritated and made a fist ready to pummel Ónu.

Ónu gave Eriri, a confused look.

"Mpa, he is still in shock."

"I've told you to stop doing that," Eriri reprimanded his offspring. He didn't seem to have a thought of his own anymore since she started reading his mind.

Ómalichanwa scrubbed the cocoyam leaf like she did her washing until it went limp then she tore it to pieces and buried it. She roused herself and said, "Mpa, you know I can't control it."

Eriri watched her wondering why she made a mould over it. Not keen on discovering the details of her intention, he turned to Ónu who looked at them morosely. Eriri wanted to, at that moment, break Ónu's head but sniped at him, "You don't know your compound?"

Ónu blinked. Ómalichanwa walked to him and rubbed his forehead and blew on it. He shuddered and opened his eyes, recovering from his shock. He peered at her and exclaimed in recognition.

"Nwó'bim!" Ónu pulled her into a crushing embrace. When she finally untangled herself, she stalked off a few paces to the left where she plucked *mgbendenji* leaves and a poisonous mushroom and gave it to Ónu.

"Eat." She commanded.

"But…"

"The leaves will neutralise the poison."

Ónu grimaced and tossed it to the ground.

She picked them up and looked into his eyes as she offered it to him again. "Eat."

He took them from her and started chewing it quickly.

Eriri watched them, amused.

"The sun will soon be up. This will renew your strength." Ómalichanwa said, rousing herself.

Ónu blinked and rubbed his cheek. "You should have

28

said that before." And took Eriri's hand as he got up.

"Who is that?" Someone cried in the distance.

"It-"

Eriri covered Ónu's mouth.

Ónu pulled Eriri's hand off. "That is my weemate!" he spat.

"Don't!" Ómalichanwa warned, glaring at them.

"You insolent youngling! How dare you?" Ónu asked in a loud whisper and returned to muttering to himself.

"Do you want me to make you dumb?" Ómalichanwa asked.

Ónu fell silent. He didn't know if she could. He wasn't even sure of what she could do. He could still see the blood when he closed his eyes and shook his head vigorously to shake it off, but it still wouldn't leave.

"Uncle," Ómalichanwa touched his shoulder gently then curtsied. "No one can know that I'm here."

He nodded and patted her head.

A few minutes later, they were neatly tucked into Ónu's newest hut, and Ónu moved to his second weemate's hut.

Soon after Ómalichanwa had started a fire, Eriri asked. "Could you have made him dumb?"

Ómalichanwa laughed. "Oh! No o! I couldn't think of anything else to say at the time."

Eriri smiled and was lost in thought. He missed Ómalichanwa, his weemate whom everyone believed he killed. She was the belle of the village, and her parents wanted her to marry into a well-known family and not the offspring of a flintsmith. When she found out she was pregnant, she ran to her grandmother's village, he ran away after her. It was the best time in their lives. There, no one interfered with their dalliance. Her grandmother had blessed their union in front of the gods, but there was the dowry to think of. As soon as the babeling was weaned, she returned to visit her parents and was locked up until the marriage rites were completed.

He wished he had been allowed to pay her dowry when she returned. Instead they sent her away in marriage to a merfolk older than her de'nnâ. She escaped and came to him, his instincts fought against letting her stay, but he loved her too much to let her go. He had gone to his de'nnâ's hut to work on more flints and came back just before high noon to give her food. He walked into his hut and picked up a bloodied flinchete just as the youths arrived at his compound. He wasn't even allowed to see her body before they carted him off.

He wondered if she would have approved of her offspring coming back to this village. She looked exactly like her nné. She would be pleased that her offspring was wise beyond her years like she was. He looked at his offspring once again and hoped she hadn't taken after her nné in stubbornness too.

"You're thinking of my nné." Ómalichanwa acknowledged smiling.

"I never got the chance to do right by her."

She was quiet for a while, staring into the fire. "Your Nwónna took care of that, but they don't know about me. For now, it's best they don't." She paused as she watched the fire crackle. "I'm glad you named me after her."

"It's what she wanted." He said and leaned back on the side of the bamboo bed.

Ómalichanwa smiled and nodded. She couldn't embarrass her de'nnâ by telling him that she could now tell when someone was telling lies. She also couldn't tell him that she was one of a triplet, especially as she didn't know if the others were still alive. Sighing, she pondered on the unfavourable omen. She only wished she had met her siblings and a part of her desperately wanted to tell him that she was the last of the triplets her nné bore.

5.

That night, after sending his special group of warriors off to Isekó and to Oche-eze's house, Okpararebisi sent for his offspring, whose name he didn't yet know. His offspring also lived in Isekó and came with his nné, Uzó. And Uzó, with four out-cast warriors.

Uzò, who was once his yoyoma, was the owner of the lewd-hut that once caused rampage in all the communities of El'ikenueze and some of their neighbours. He wilfully sent her on exile, because he discovered that he'd built the lewd-huts by himself under her spell and had a babeling which she claimed had died at birth. Uzó was his grandmother's best friend although his late nné's age mate, a widow from her youth. She was married to his grandfather's nwónnenanna who fell into the lake and was never seen again. She wasn't beautiful, but she was envied by her peers regardless because she had a body that beckoned even the strongest-willed merfolk. The first time he'd met her was the day after his second Imaonyemgbu rite. To keep his bullying nwónnenanna at bay, he would go and sit with his granny and Uzò would call him 'my namesake' then carry him on her laps but she'd stopped visiting after his granny died.

This was forty cycles ago.

Okpararebisi winced and got up to stretch his achy weak bones. He had never met his de'nnâ but learned that his de'nnâ had gone fishing and never returned. To secure the throne, his grandfather King Anyanwuze adopted three of his nephews as his other wives bore him no babeling.

I will not make my grandfather's mistake. My nephews had lined up in wait. I knew an uprising was imminent, so

I took care of them before ascending this throne. If only that infernal cousin of mine were born in this palace kingdom, I would have found him before he was discovered.

He suspected some of the elders knew of his atrocities, but as none dared to confront him, he dismissed it. The elders and marshals were like the tail of the lizard that always grew back, but that was what they were, tails.

He was good at taking care of his problems from when he was a youngling. His uncles were nefarious merfolks, and his grandfather was oblivious to what went on in his household. Tired of being hungry, he began to blackmail the maids that constantly had *private meetings* with his uncles, and the problem was solved. It was that same day that he discovered that he didn't need to wait on anyone else to take care of his problems. But age! Age had dealt a blow to that regiment.

He sighed and reminisced.

The bullying became much worse after his first rite of passage. His nwónnenanna put together knew just a third of the proverbs and the morals of every story their grandfather had ever told them, and his grandfather compared his success with his elder nwónnenanna and cousins; no youngling his age had ever completed the Imaonyemgbu not to talk of the Imanwoke.

On one occasion, after his nwónnenanna had bullied him for hours, he decided to go to the lakeside. On his way, he met a very pretty youngling and walked with her. She was the one that gave him the ideas that helped him excel in the Imaonyemgbu and the Imanwoke rites concurrently. The one youngling he truly cared about. A youngling that would have been his weemate if people weren't so nosy.

He continued to visit the lakeside even when she no

longer visited and long after the lake had dried up. Then one day, he decided to check a new path through Rumuoriji; halfway through, he saw a bird; produced his catapult and searched for a stone simultaneously. Finding one, he walked to it and was about to pick it up when he heard whistling. He thinned his lips, a deep frown set on his face, intent on knowing who had such a voice, he set out in search of it. He climbed a tree to get a better view. In his search, he noticed a movement and then heard water splash. Startled, he lost his grip and balance and toppled down the hill. Plantain trees broke his descent. Feeling no pain, he sighed with relief and was about to raise himself when a hand tugged him up by the ear.

"I'm sorry. I didn't mean to -"

"Close your eyes!" A harsh voice commanded. A few seconds later, the voice murmured, "Open your eyes."

He opened them slowly and exclaimed, "My grandmother's friend, greetings!" He curtsied to her.

She stood towering over him, trying to look intimidating with arms akimbo and an eyebrow jutting up. "And you are?"

"Uzò, the last born of Jiriehui." He got up slowly. She seemed to have grown shorter than the last time he'd seen her.

"The one named after me. How are you young one?" she asked with a small smile.

"I'm fine," Okpararebisi said as he lowered his head shyly.

"Why have you wandered so far from El'ikenueze?"

He looked up at her, confused, and she explained, "You are in Rumuoriji. No royal ventures out of El'ikenueze without a guard."

Okpararebisi frowned. He didn't understand why she would say that. He'd been told that there was no

33

demarcation in the lands. More so, he had never even seen a guard, and why would he need one? They were all equals. Each merfolk's reign was within his compound -everyone knew this. It was once rumoured that she had gone mad after the death of her husband. It was probably true because she lived in the forest. Worried, he looked around furtively for an escape route. The area didn't look much like a forest, but he had to leave as soon and as quietly as possible. Why would his grandmother be friends with a mad person? Maybe they weren't really friends.

"My grandmother's best friend, can you please show me the way home?" He asked, smiling sweetly. He wanted to ensure he didn't provoke her so she wouldn't bite him – a mad person's bite was believed to lead the victim to madness.

"Of course. But first, a guest must wash their hands to join in the festivity of the soup pot."

Okpararebisi looked around. He heard no drums, no music, nor did he see people. "I hear no celebration -"

"It is a parable, young one. It is only in your enemy's house that you do not eat what is served you. And yet, even that is a taboo."

Okpararebisi gulped and nodded. What do mad people eat? He pondered.

"But first, you must clean up," she murmured and gestured.

He looked down and noticed the mud caking on his clothing. His grandfather would not be pleased, not when there was a celebration and he was wearing the only ceremonial ensemble he had. He looked up at her, embarrassed, but she casually pointed to a large ité-mini and then to a small one with a calabash beside it. He used the calabash to fill the smaller ité-mini. He had never washed without the servants assisting, but he knew what

34

to do. He just had to wait until she had gone away. When she didn't move, he decided to wash off the mud from just his hides.

She shook her head and went away.

When he finished, he replaced the pot and calabash and followed the path she had taken. It led to an ample open space, and ahead of him was a tent whose thatched roof needed repair. Underneath was an ité on the fire and beside it was a freshly roasted fish splayed on cocoyam leaves. There was a very small pot of palm oil beside it. No one was supposed to dig up their yams until after the harvest blessings on the eve of the new yam festival, but the smell of cooking yam wafted through his nostril, and his stomach responded.

He shrugged. It was only abominable if someone noticed, eh? She was mad, he was hungry, and she wasn't cooking mud.

She cleared her throat, and he spun quickly.

"Here. Put these on. They used to belong to my husband, but you will manage it until yours are dry."

Okpararebisi didn't think his grandfather would approve not because he was a youngling of sixteen cycles but because he'd preached; 'take not food, hide or land belonging to another no matter how desperately you desire it'. He shrugged again, feeling justified because he didn't beg or ask; she offered, and it would be insolent to reject a kind offer. Besides, a few hours away from his nwónnenanna would do him some good. He went to the back, changed, and was back a few minutes later.

"Let me take care of that," She insisted with a small smile and took his wet garments from him.

Okpararebisi grinned bashfully and nodded to himself. It was nice to be treated like a prince sometimes. Her late husband's clothes were snug and soft, really soft. If she *continued like this, she would give him a reason to stop by more often. When she returned, she was carrying a large gourd and two little ones. The top of the large one cradled a nest of grass. He knew right away; it was palm wine. He thought he'd die of bliss and licked his lips just as she handed him a gourd filled with the frothy white liquid. Ever since he tasted it at his cousin Akudo's wedding ceremony, he'd longed for the fresh, sweet and smooth liquid.*

After a few more gourds, he began to feel dizzy. He got up and staggered wedging himself between the stool and the wood supporting the tent then passed out. He woke up a while later to find himself naked beside his grandmother's friend.

Startled, he shrieked, waking her. She smiled and caressed his phallus. He tried to move away, but her hand was firm, and his will failed him. In a blink, she was on top of him.

By the time he got back to the palace, it was dusk. He saw masked merfolks beside his grandfather's hut. They all had flinchetes in their hands and small flint tied with a string of leather around their legs; they wore glistening hides around their waists, and all had a fur sash across their shoulders. Three had tall feathers on their head held together by a string. The others kept a palm frond between their lips.

6.

His grandfather beckoned him into his hut. He began to shiver. The last time he was in trouble his grandfather warned him that he was going to sell him off so as soon as he entered the hut, he knelt to plead with his grandfather, but his grandfather gave him a stern look and

36

commanded. "Sit down with your siblings."

He looked at his siblings, then at his de'nnâ's nwónne, Omehia, Nwóna'azu, and Cheta and frowned. Everyone was present except...

"Your granny has just joined our ancestors, and the light has gone from my heart. My time is equally near. You will, all of you have to be strong these few days. I need to determine who'll be the caretaker of the Ófòr-Oguneli. You, offshoots of my offspring will be confined to your quarters and will come out only at my bidding. The palace guards are not here for your protection but to carry out their duties. They are to ensure everyone adheres to my instructions as tradition demands."

Omehia looked around uncomfortably. He cleared his throat and asked. "How many moons do you need to deliberate?"

"Four. You and your nwónnenanna are also not permitted to leave these premises."

Omehia, Nwóna'azu and Cheta bowed and chorused, "Yes De'nnâ."

He waved them off, and everyone got up to leave. "Uzò!"

Okpararebisi froze in his tracks. Fidgeting as he awaited his punishment.

"Where are you coming from?"

Okpararebisi lowered his head, he couldn't possibly mention where he'd been and what he'd been up to as it all spelt taboo.

His grandfather cleared his throat expectantly.

"I went to the stream to clear my head."

"Hmm," the king paused and beckoned him. When he approached the king looked at him, concern and worry written on his face, then he rested a hand on Okpararebisi's shoulder and said; "A seed that is not dead cannot birth a tree. You've got to grow a thick hide. Where have you heard *that running away solved anything, eh? Now, go join your siblings."*

That night, his siblings bullied him even more, but he didn't care. His mind was fixed on his next visit to Uzò, his granny's best friend's hut. She had given him permission to call her by her name. His grandfather will be in mourning and will also be confined to his quarters in deliberation. All he had to do was get past the guards unnoticed. He would also have to bribe his bath-maids. And he would also have to wake up much earlier than his siblings.

And he did so.

He was at Uzò's until it was almost dawn. He snuck back into the palace just as the maids were coming to prepare him for his bath as they had arranged. He dispatched two uncompromising maids. While he took his bath, he heard a commotion, he didn't bother coming out. It wasn't like he was ever expected to do anything or that anything he did was appreciated. Besides, he was tired of playing peacemaker and getting bullied for it. It was probably one of his uncles' weemate's feignings or allegings that had started the one thing or another to get their husbands into fighting each other again.

Like an approaching torrent, scream after scream then wailing ensued.

"Something is wrong," he cried, nudging the maid scrubbing him away. Draped haphazardly in his hide, he hurried to the hut he shared with his siblings as quickly as he could. When he got to the gathering, he shoved past to see what they were all staring at. It was his uncles, Nwóna'azu and Cheta, lying in precarious positions in pools of their blood in front of his hut. Some of the guards had blood on their flinchetes. He never liked his uncles anyway; there was no love lost between them and were only cordial when their grandparents were within ears-

reach.

What he couldn't fathom was why his uncles were dressed like the guards of last night. He made to enter the hut, but a guard blocked the entrance just as one of the guards with feathers in his headpiece ran through the group that circled him panting. Between pants, he whispered into Okpararebisi's ear.

"The King demands your presence, my prince." The guard with the headpiece whispered.

Okpararebisi looked back at the hut and shrugged, he would just be bullied again anyway. He let out a sigh of defeat. It was too late to make his escape to rendezvous with Uzò. He bowed in curtsy to his grandfather, who was dressed in the full regalia of a King. He frowned and looked around. All the elders were present in full regalia complete with their insignia. He peered at the crowd. His siblings were not there neither was Omehia. His grandfather looked on stoically when he turned to face Okpararebisi, then watched him intently, Okpararebisi was about to confess when his grandfather summoned his counsel to dress Okpararebisi.

Oche-Eze, the Chief Priest raised a hand to stop King Anyanwuze. King Anyanwuze rebuked Oche-Eze with a frown. Oche-Eeze blinked intently. Exasperated, King Anyanwuze shrugged and gestured.

"Come forward childling," Oche-Eze murmured and rumbled through his sack bag.

Okpararebisi cautiously walked towards Oche-Eze silently praying that his secret remained his.

"I have a few questions to put to you. There are grave consequences to these actions and because Evovuotu's future rests in a pure sitting on that throne. You must answer them as honestly as possible. You can ask questions or explain, understand?"

Okpararebisi nodded.

Oche-Eze glared at him.

"Yes," Okpararebisi said solemnly.

"Yes, I understand," Oche-Eze corrected.

"Yes, I understand," Okpararebisi retorted.

"Have you spilled blood?"

"Yes."

"Human blood."

"No."

"Have you told a lie that has resulted in the exile of another from this clan?"

"No."

"From this community?"

"No."

"From this kingdom?"

"No."

"Have you visited the loins of weefolk, with or without a betroth, or in a lewd house?"

"No."

"Have you entered into an agreement with any god or spirit?"

"No."

"Have you without permission touched Ófòr-Nkigwe or Ófòr-Oguneli?"

"No."

"Have you tasted sweet wine?"

"No."

"Shall we proceed?" King Anyanwuze smiled coldly at Oche-Eze.

"Yes," Oche-Eze muttered, rolling his eyes then gestured at Okpararebisi. "Go and kneel before your King."

As soon as he was dressed in full regalia of a crown prince, Oche-Eze got up. Even with his cane, Oche-Eze was still bent double; and although he wasn't old, he always looked grumpy. His wiry grey and white hair shaped like limp spikes. There were three white lines drawn on each arm, and half of his face was painted white, the other black. He produced a flint that was as clear as water and as flat as a leaf then started chanting. As soon as Oche-Eze started chanting, everyone in the hut quickly scrambled for a place to sit as quietly as they could. The ceremony was quick and solemn.

Okpararebisi was adorned with the totem cape of kingship which made him itch, then handed him the Ófòr-Nkigwe and then the Ófòr-Oguneli. Immediately after, his grandfather introduced him to the Imperial Guard. The warriors' flinchetes were red, flat, and broad. The marshals were the ones in feathers, and their flinchetes were red, thin and slender. The Lord Marshal had died weeks before, and it wasn't time to crown anyone for that position as it had to be earned.

The duty now fell on him. King Anyanwuze blessed his only surviving offshoot and sent him away.

Okpararebisi left with the Imperial Guard. They were to take him to a secure location in Rumujieli. When they got to the outskirts of El'ikenueze on the ridge just outside Rumuoriji, the warriors decided to rest as they hadn't slept in days. By right, they were not to stop until they arrived at their destination. They sent a few servants to get them food. None came back except one, he was carting a large raffia bag tied to two long sticks. Soon after they were served, they gulped and slurped their food.

Okpararebisi had no appetite. Worry had replaced hunger; he was worried about the implication of what his grandfather and the Chief Priest had said after he'd told them he had not known the loins of a weefolk, tasted sweet wine or done any abominable act. Well, if it were true, he should have gone mad the instant they'd adorned him with the totem cape. He could now marry Chinasa if he ever found her. He could wait until she was found, after all, he was now king. He couldn't marry Uzò even if he wanted to. She was a widow, without child, and he was almost half her age. He just wanted her body as she reminded him of his Chinasa.

He was still lost in thought when he heard an uproar. The warriors were groping their stomachs in pain and looking for the servant who had purchased the food. One of the merfolks who kept watch ran back to inform them that they were in danger, but it was too late. From behind Okpararebisi, one of the Marshals grabbed him roughly and told him to run and not look back. He did as he was told, holding the bag the Marshal had given him. He ran close to the path but not on it. He stopped under a large tree as he tried to assess where he was. Recognising the tree, he quickly changed into the outfit in the bag and ran towards Uzò's hut.

He inhaled deeply, holding his breath as he knocked on the window at the back of the house.

Uzó peered through the crack of her straw window, pulled back and peered again. Surprised to see him return so soon she hesitated to open the door, but only briefly. When she cracked the door open, he slid in, forcing her to step out of the way. She quickly closed it after him and folded her arm across her body.

He assumed her reaction was because she wanted to sleep as they'd been up all night.

But Uzó was hiding from the servant she'd sold sleeping treatments to, knowing it was poison.

Okpararebisi pushed her to the bed, and when he was done, he sat up and said, "My siblings were murdered before I got back this morning."

She gasped noisily and crawled towards him. "I'm so sorry," she drawled, massaging his neck and shoulders.

"Now, I'm supposed to find the next Chieftain of Divinity, Wealth & Duty." He roused himself from the bed and began to pace, one hand rubbing his shaven chin. "How am I supposed to find out who that is? The only person that knew how to get me to this unknown person died on our way there. How...?" He looked at her longingly and shook his head. "Put something on. You're distracting me."

7.

Uzò rolled her eyes but didn't budge. She walked to the window and stared out.

"Did you not hear a thing I said? Why are you still naked?" He inquired frowning.

"Your Majesty, I long for you." she purred, repeatedly blinking as she sauntered towards him.

He smiled. "You don't have to try so hard. I do however have to think."

Uzó sighed disdainfully. 'So do I, you insolent youngling! You're more than a merfolk, but you think like a childling. I'm tired of being lonely, and you'll be useful, very useful. I best pay another visit to that disgusting old merfolk. He owed me a favour, and I need a love potion.'

Okpararebisi tilted his head, concerned he said, "You seem distracted."

Uzò sighed despairingly.

"What is it?"

She shrugged.

"Out with it!" Okpararebisi grimaced.

Uzò looked up absentmindedly. "I can see a gap in the roof. The rain is fast approaching to water the seedlings in the ground. My hands aren't firm enough to build..."

"Get someone to fix it!"

"I'll do that right away." She said and quickly dressed up. She returned just before sunset. Instead of welcoming her, he demanded food. He seemed comfortable walking around the compound naked, and it gave her an idea. A cantankerous idea and now that the herbs the disgusting old merfolk's love portion was about to be erased. She could already see the money piling in. She prepared his meal and added a new one.

Okpararebisi ate the food with relish. Not long after he gawked at her, longingly. The disgust had worn off.

She pouted and feigned sorrow.

"Out with it!" Okpararebisi ordered, casually.

Uzò sighed ruefully. "The rain is fast approaching to water the seedlings in the ground."

"And what of it?" Okpararebisi asked a little irritated and looking back at the hut with only one thing in mind.

"Your Majesty, I have no seed to plant. I can't fix leaking roof much less hire work hands."

"Say no more. I'll start to take care of it. Tomorrow, I'll get the raffia."

"But Your Majesty, your safety?" She queried feigning concern as she demurely arched her back. "Why don't I go out there and get it. Then you can... your majesty I."

"I like the way you say it."

She smiled with a crinkle around her eyes. "Say what, Your Majesty?"

"Show me some love."

She was exhausted from visiting the old merfolk, but he'd warned her of this. She submitted herself to his wanton desires while she daydreamed of her coming wealth.

Moons and Sunshines passed into seasons while Okpararebisi was in Uzò's compound. He had finished the roof and plastered the hut, built her a food-hut, repaired the cooking-tent, a large bath-hut, two new huts and replaced her hut with a hut big enough for a large family. He had hewn seats from the tree that lightning felled days ago. As soon as the sunset, before the moon rose, weefolks would come in the pretext of visiting her, and she would offer him to them in exchange for wares. She always made sure that on such days, he didn't step out of the hut and the raffia windows remained down no matter how hot the weather got. These he did all by himself. Anything to make her happy.

One day, while he was still smoothing the surface of the seats, he felt an uncontrollable urge to throw up. It was like something clung to the insides of his throat, and he couldn't get it out. It was suffocating him. No matter how much water he drank, he just couldn't bring it out. He went into the food-hut to get palm oil and salt and mixed it as his grandfather had taught him. After he'd drunk it, he began to strike his chest, and a few minutes later, he puked out an egg. A whole black egg which made a splat on reaching the ground. His grandfather had told him that only charms had that effect.

As he was contemplating on who could have done it to him, he noticed something odd at the corner of the food-hut. It was a doll in the replica of a living folk. He would have ignored it but for the fact that it had his insignia. He picked it up and pulled a straw from the head of it. Heat rose in his scalp, a searing pain much like something was being pulled out of his head. He quickly soaked doll in palm oil and ran to the back of the house with a flint, cut open the stalk of one of the plantain trees and tucked the doll inside it. A while later, he retrieved the doll, took it with

45

him to the cooking-tent, started a fire, and tossed the doll in. As soon as it was ash, a weight fell off his shoulder. A sense of awareness surged through him then his mind reeled as memories flooded his mind. It began with the warrior telling him to run. He shook violently until he passed out.

When he came through, he appraised himself. He was muscular, had a beard and was dressed in rags. There were many changes in the compound. He had no recollection of what happened after he entered Uzò's hut on that fateful day. *I need to get to the Ófòr-Oguneli as soon as possible. I hope I can remember the uncloaking spell.* He went to the back of the enormous hut he suspected was the position of the old hut in search of the totem cape, regalia, Ófòr-Oguneli, and Ófòr-Nkigwe he'd hidden. He lifted the sceptres. They looked exactly as he'd left them. After digging up half of the back of the enormous hut, he found them covered in stiffened sand, his regalia and totem cape had decayed and was completely ridden with worms. He shook the worms off. Energy passed through his hands and sparkled where his fingertips touched the regalia, and it started to renew itself. He smiled as he felt his strength increase. He thought of a flinchete and in a flash, he was in the food-hut beside his flinchete. Shaking off, his dizzying. He laughed maniacally. He'd heard stories but he was living the dream.

He was glad that he never got the chance to hand the Ófòr-Oguneli to its successor. For the power he felt could only have come from it. He dusted the rags he had on, and it was restored to its former glory. It was the same hide she had given him the first time they'd met, and it was too tight, so he blew on the bodice, and it enlarged to fit his bulk. He wondered what was happening in his grandfather's compound. Suddenly, he saw the palace; it felt like he was running but his feet didn't move. He blinked and felt like someone had pulled him and he was awake. No one could run that fast. He shrugged it off and blinked. He was still standing with his flinchete in hand. It dawned on him that he hadn't moved. He suspected that it was how Oche-Eze discovered culprits.

He nodded to himself. It was like his grandfather had said; 'you think of anything, and you get it except you couldn't control another living folk'. He inhaled and held his breath as he came into his grandfather's compound again. His uncle sat on the throne; his head hung low. At first, he thought his uncle was dead, but then he heard snoring. Some elders were with him laughing and clicking their palm wine gourds. None of them drank from the small gourds in front of them. A few elders he recognised, but all were in a pensive mood. He withdrew and was back in his body.

Feeling exhausted, he laid back on the bamboo bed. He sat up and looked around fingering the frame. He had singlehandedly built his Uzò a palace. She must have known that he would never willingly give up the throne. He stared at his hand, grinning. He could give her a swift punishment.

He thought of the palace and was back in the throne room. While he was trying to figure out how to coerce secrets out of his uncle, he heard a weefolk scream. He took his mind to the sound. It was coming out of one of his late uncle's hut, and he didn't think it would be a good idea to go in there, so he waited as it was supposed to be private. Around the compound, two childlings were playing. One was the replica of the other except where one was fair-skinned the other was dark-skinned. They were girl childlings. They looked up at someone and called her, 'nné'. He frowned and followed them as they ran to the weefolk.

47

It was Cheta, nwónnenanna's weemate. He was stunned because they didn't have childlings or even babelings when he was still in the palace.

"How many cycles of seasons have I been under Uzò's spell? What has happened to my grandfather? Did they think I was dead?"

He came back to himself and would have lost balance if he wasn't sitting down. His head throbbed. The childlings playing looked no less than three cycles. The thought that he had no control over his actions made him violently angry. Ready to kill her with his bare hands, he wondered where he could find her. As the thought formed in his mind, he saw footprints; they glistened, a waft of brown smoke seemed to be emanating from the footprints and faded. He followed them.

These footprints, he suspected, were one of the powers attributed to the Paramount Ruler of War and Servitude. He followed them until he got to the market and found her haggling. He watched her weigh a bunch of pumpkin leaves. He stood beside her, and she jerked her head back like she had seen him. She looked through him, frowned, shrugged and returned to her haggling. He nodded his approval; this could come in handy. He smiled and raised his hand to her neck when a childling tugged its nné pointed at him.

Startled, he retreated to himself. His head was beginning to whirl from the numerous powers within him, some threatening to burst, and his body felt like it was being pricked all over. He was hungry, sweaty, itchy and ticklish, his eyes hurt, and his body felt like an iroko tree had been used to pummel him. How did the childling recognise me? Did an Okoruchi recognise another Okoruchi? Would I recognise them?

As he pondered, he heard a babeling laughter, a

48

babeling cry, and he gasped and tapped his head, and the fragmented memory tried to reveal itself.

We had babelings! He shook his head.

"No! she had an offspring, a girl childling who came to visit from time to time. And yes, we had a babeling, but it died. The day it died, I heard her talk to someone. The merfolk had come to help bury it. Why didn't I meet the merfolk? I was drunk! Why was I drunk? Because of the loss? No, I wasn't drunk. It's what she said to the merfolk. I had to do something for her. It had to do with food. Why couldn't I leave the hut?"

He moaned and reneged. She was once the nné of his childling, and so he decided not to kill her, but that her punishment would be a long odious one and he would wait until he could unleash a suitable one for stealing his opportunity of finding Chinasa, his love.

He stepped outside again, and the overwhelming smells of greenery almost knocked the air out of his lungs. Their scents were both intoxicating and scintillating; as they wrapped around him, his throat itched, his eyes watered and his nostrils, clogged. They felt... alive! *How can plants be alive?* Each plant had its own scent, and they seemed to be greeting him, introducing themselves and their attributes.

An idea occurred to him. He followed the scent of the flowers and plants he needed. He went as far as the thicket of the forest to get the exact nectar he needed to add to the items he had already collected. He didn't understand how but he knew what was required as he zipped in and out of the forest in a blur, then separated the items. One set he squeezed the juice into her bathwater and lined all clay pots in the house. Another he added to her favourite soup. He desperately wanted to add it to her palm wine, but she had a good nose. Wanting her to think he was coming back, *he left his flinchete. From then on Uzò retained her youth but remained unapproachable.*

He stepped out again. As he did, the overwhelming aromas and fragrances of greenery almost knocked the air out of his lungs. Their scents were both intoxicating and scintillating; as they wrapped around him, his throat itched, his eyes watered and his nostrils, clogged. They felt, alive! How can plants be alive? He knew plants were alive, but he could feel them the way you'd feel standing by a living folk. Each plant had its own scent, and they seemed to be greeting him, introducing themselves and their attributes.

An idea occurred to him. He followed the scent of the flowers and plants he needed. He went as far as the thicket of the forest to get the exact nectar he needed, the exact nut, the juice of an exact budding flower, the bark of an exact tree to create a special set of potions. He didn't understand how but he knew what was required as he zipped in and out of the forest in a blur, then separated the items. One set he squeezed their juice into her bathwater and lined all clay pots in the house. Another he added to her favourite soup. He desperately wanted to add it to her palm wine, but she had a good nose. Wanting her to think he was coming back, he left his flinchete. From then on Uzò retained her youth but remained unapproachable.

It took him two moons to get to El'ikenueze. When he arrived at the palace, he thought of being invisible and looked down and almost laughed out loud because it had worked. He went to the back of the house and hid under the shrubby tree which he used to stay in to hide from his siblings. It had been a perfect hideout until they started tying rats to strings and hang them around the tree to attract snakes. The flood of memories made the scenery eerie. Apart from him, only one heir to the throne was alive, his uncle Omehia. It didn't take him long to discover that Omehia was the murderer. He got so angry that he wanted to quieten the scream coming out of his late uncle, Nwóna'azu's hut. He went in - though not leaving the spot under the tree - and found Nwóna'azu's widow crying.

"I don't want this accursed babeling!" Nwóna'azu's weemate screamed.

The old weefolk who was helping her birth the babeling slapped her across her cheek.

"Please don't come out. You deserve a better de'nnâ. Don't come out!" Nwóna'azu's weemate pleaded with the babeling in her womb.

"Taah! Don't say such things," the old weefolk hissed as she held out her hands to welcome the babeling. He remembered the birther well, he didn't at first. She was his Chinasa's mistress.

As soon as the babeling came out, Okpararebisi touched its head and then its nné's. A maid had already gone to tell the King that it was a boy babeling when it stopped crying. The birther checked the babeling and froze. Its nné's head fell back with relief. The birther checked the nné's pulse and covered her mouth, so she wouldn't scream. Okpararebisi smiled bashfully. He couldn't wait to see how she was going to explain herself to the king.

He was thoughtful for a while and decided he didn't want to kill his nwónnenanna right away. Instead, he would watch him suffer until he confessed to killing the entire royal family. Okpararebisi headed for the palace just as the second maid was running towards it with the sad news. He raised a brow at one of the cohorts whom he was going to torment at dusk then returned to his body. In that instant, he was hit with the incredible urge to urinate and excrete at the same time. At the same time, he heard lingering footsteps. Peering out of his hideout, he could only make out a silhouette and only remembered there were insects when he heard clapping and watched the silhouette's hand movements. A few seconds passed and another set of footsteps approached, faster, holding a gourd-lanthorn.

"Nné, you're late," the silhouette with the gourd-lanthorn muttered as they hurriedly embraced each other.

Okpararebisi strained his ears to hear what they were saying even though his focus was on the silhouette with the gourd-lanthorn because her scent ensnared him. It was difficult to control his urge to urinate, listen in, and try to make out their faces at the same time.

"Nwô'm, how are you?" The muffled voice, though familiar, was muffled.

The youngling said nothing but looked surreptitiously around.

"You have news?" Her nné asked.

"It was a boy childling."

Her nné froze with eyes that looked like they were about to pop while her mouth hung open.

"It died. It came out alive and just died," the youngling added with a hint of horror in her voice.

"Our ancestors have heard our prayers," her nné clasped her hands in excitement.

"That's beside the point, when do I get to leave? I do not like how His Majesty looks at me." The youngling sputtered, sounding annoyed.

Her nné smiled, glad that the charm worked but annoyed at her daughter's reluctance. "But why? You are the fairest maiden in all the lands combined."

"But Nné, my heart beats for another."

"It's been five cycles already, forget him. He hasn't been back since he fed the warriors their last meal."

"Which you provided," the youngling spat and slapped her hand, almost knocking down the torch.

"Oh, he knew what he was getting himself into," her nné said firmly

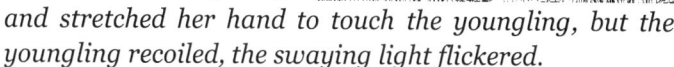

and stretched her hand to touch the youngling, but the youngling recoiled, the swaying light flickered.

"You poisoned them, Nné. How am I sure -?"

"Shut up!" Her nné hissed. "The night has not lost its ears."

"Did you kill him too?" The youngling asked in a loud whisper.

"I did not," her nné retorted firmly.

"Nné -"

"Forget him," her nné warned coldly.

"Like you forgot my de'nnâ?"

The weefolk slapped the youngling and pulled her close almost immediately.

"Avenge your de'nnâ, and the boy will return."

"Nné, I'm tired of this!" The youngling grumbled disdainfully.

"You watch your tone. This was your idea, was it not?"

The youngling fell silent.

"You've got to finish what you started," the nné said softly. "You can achieve whatever you set your mind to, even if it is the King. Your de'nnâ would be proud of you."

"You made me -"

"Enough! Now go be a good offspring. You need enough rest for your chores tomorrow."

The youngling gritted her teeth as her nné turned to leave and spun around. Shaking her head, she began to leave.

"Offspring of mine," the weefolk called.

The youngling stopped in her tracks but didn't turn around.

"If he wants you, let him have you," her nné said in a strange voice then added sternly. "And when he does, come to me."

The weefolk paused dramatically, causing the youngling to turn around.

Her nné smiled and nodded curtly. "You will give him an heir and we'll take the Kingdom which rightfully belonged to your de'nnâ."

Seeing tears streamed down the youngling's face, the weefolk walked to her, wiped her tears with the back of her hands, and cupped her face.

"Remember! You can share your bed without sharing your heart. Do not forget your de'nnâ. Take back what was his," her nné let out an exasperated sigh. "Now, cry no more. Think less, my dear. We have a family to conquer and a throne to retrieve."

The youngling nodded.

"I have a guest, and I don't want him to get suspicious."

"Who?" the youngling asked, suspiciously.

"He is useful," the nné patted her offspring's shoulder impatiently. "No one to concern yourself with, eh! Now go!"

8.

Okpararebisi couldn't make out who they were. The youngling's nné had something on her that repelled him because he had not felt the invisible wall until the weefolk arrived. No matter how hard he tried to break through the barrier between them, he couldn't so he waited to look and ended up urinating on himself. He tried to imagine being beside both weefolks, but a force shoved him away. It left him startled and somewhat afraid because his mind didn't only return to his body, but he materialised at the bath-hut he once shared with his siblings.

Now, he knew the warriors were killed by a widow whose offspring worked as a maid in the palace and that he'd missed being poisoned by a stroke of luck. Now, he needed to know if she was the same person who murdered his siblings and his grandpapa as it seemed Omehia, like himself, may have also escaped by a stroke of luck. For all he knew the youngling he'd seen could have been one of the maids that bathed him. Her nné had obscured her face from his view. The realisation that there was an enemy in the palace made him desire foreknowledge to ensure that he'll not be killed in the quest to take back his throne. Hungry, tired, and stinking of urine, the stirrings of his loin baffled him.

He grimaced as he remembered he was also thinking of taking a bath. The large bath house needed repairs; grass protruded from the ground and from the cracks on the walls. The walls had lent itself to wildflowers and there were heaps of fallen leaves on the ground in various stages of decay. He had to have been the last person to use it, he thought. The thought gave him some discomfort. He thought of what to do, he griped. He was hungry and dirty; he couldn't go to the food hut or fetch water. Given the chance, he wouldn't know where to go. The large ité-mini still had water in it. He tasted it and spat in disgust at the vile taste. Morosely he stared at the water then a nimbus glowed. It was the same one he'd used to get the herbs earlier.

He felt like he was being pulled in three directions; a yellow nimbus pulled his left hand towards the ité-mini, the green nimbus pulled him right towards the mushrooms growing near broken shards of ions; a yellow nimbus pulled his left hand towards an ité-mini and the algae in the shards, a brown nimbus tugged his head to the side towards unfamiliar sounds - all these happened in seconds and at the same time. His legs dragged behind him, then his heart sank to his stomach when he saw an apparition. Appalled by the odour it exuded, he shrunk. It seemed to be beckoning him. He shook his head. He was going to die but not now. He wasn't old enough. As the apparition neared, others appeared with outstretched arms. His entire body shuddered violently. The closer they got, the colder he felt. There were so many voices that his ears from within his head were drumming. His forehead felt very hot. In an instant, the voices, the cold and even the apparition were gone. He opened his eyes, touched his body to see if he was intact while trying to focus his vision. It was still dark and quiet except for the night owl, the cuckoo and the cricket.

He hadn't been made aware of a nimbus for the gateway to the great beyond. He always thought it was a myth because his grandfather had made no mention of it.

Although the events that had taken place since sun-up had confounded him, this topped it all. It also helped him realise that there was more to the Ófòr-Oguneli than met the eyes. He made a mental note to explore it.

Seconds later, he heard voices, talking and laughing, followed by a few squabbles. There was a slight difference in their voices. Where one sounded like tapping, the other sounded like squeaking. He moved closer to see who it was, making sure he was invisible. There was no one. For a moment he assumed the person was cloaked in invisibility like himself and focused on finding the exact spot the person was. In trying to stay focus on the sound, he noticed that the leaves and the stalks of the plants around him had doubled in size and was still growing. He gasped into his hands when he saw six-legged creatures in a straight line. A taller six-legged reddish-brown creature stood apart barking orders.

"Because you're ants does not give you the license to nuisance. Speed up!"

He blinked, a little startled then slanted his head to the squabble and realised it was between a mouse and a rat. The rat told a group of three mice that they were not of the same class and where not expected to be seen together. He sniggered, wondering why he would need that nimbus. He covered his ears to keep the noise out, but it didn't work so he turned to take his leave when his foot got stuck in a water pot. He had forgotten why he was there in the first place. The smell of urine brought him back to his predicament. He looked up. Seeing the plantain trees, he figured he could roast some for dinner. He tried to unsheathe his flinchete and remembered that he'd abandoned at Uzò's. Thinking of her made the stirrings in his loin feel much worse, and he groaned in frustration just as his stomach rumbled.

"I have to quell it somehow," he mused.

He whisked his hand, and two bunches of plantain fell. One of them smelt sweet; its skin was yellow and soft and looked rotten. He tasted it and moaned; it was soft and sweet. Enjoying it, he consumed almost half of the bunch. He tidied up with a flick of his hand when he heard the rustling of leaves. Relieved, he leaned against the wall of the bath-hut plucked a few leaves and dipped them in the ité-mini to purify the stagnant water and then dunked flowers into the same water as an afterthought.

After taking his bath, he felt light but smelled like flowers. He sniffed again and wrinkled his nose - he smelt like a weefolk. Chinasa would have loved it though he couldn't stand it, and worse still, it made him sneeze. Although he was exhausted, he followed the scent of the silhouette he'd seen with her mother earlier. Her scent was everywhere, and it was difficult to choose the most recent, so he followed all. He finally found her ten minutes later. She was humming as she strode in the direction of the bath-hut at the other end of the compound then vied in the opposite direction, a few paces ahead of him with a large ité-mini in the crook of her arm and a torch in the other.

It was only when she started undressing that he realised it was where the maids took their bath. Watching her further aroused him. Not used to following his instinct, he willed himself to look away as he pondered. Indecision wavered into intent, and in a flick of his fingers, the fire in the torch went out.

She hissed then rummaged in the dark for the flints which were stashed in her sack of pomander then cussed when she accidentally knocked the bag over. He pulled her roughly to himself and had his way with her. She had put up a good fight and bit off his ear. He knew she would use it to catch him out, but he knew he could heal himself. In fact, he was sure he could heal himself until he tried. Failing, he thought of the herbs that would help, and the nimbus rose through him. It was a painful experience.

As the pain lingered, he went to the hut he once shared with his siblings. Memories of them came flooding in his mind as if they were still there, causing him to be restless. There was a film of dust in the room which he swiped away with a wave of his hand and fell into a fitful sleep filled with memories of all the past Hierarchies. Not long after, he woke up shaking violently. Desiring to evade the nightmares, he went out of the hut and paced around the compound glad for the cloak of the night sky. He raised a brow and smiled knowingly when he heard groaning from his uncle's hut and shrugged. A few minutes later, he saw a maid he had never met walk towards the palace. She looked around surreptitiously and slipped in via the rear entrance of the King's court. He wanted to use his mind to see what she was up to but remembering how exhausted it had left him, he decided to stick with his invisibility.

He didn't need to go inside to hear his uncle's voice. Suspicious, he went to the hut he'd heard the coupling and almost laughed when he realised that his uncle's weemate had been with someone else. Curious to know who it was, he entered her hut, the merfolk on her was her acclaimed cousin. A while after he entered the room, the merfolk left. He flicked his hand, and the door opened and closed, but she didn't react; it seemed she was expecting someone else. So, he saw it as another opportunity to quell his hunger for Uzò, which was fast becoming a pain. An insidious pain tinged with obsession.

He had just finished with her when the merfolk returned. He shook his head; the rumours about her insatiable desires were now confirmed. It was tit for tat as her husband was no different. He came back to her twice *that night, and she didn't flinch. She knew he was different and begged him to come back again. So long as it would keep him from going back to Uzó, he didn't mind. He didn't understand why he longed for Uzó even after the spell had been broken.*

In the early hours of the new day, he returned to the hut he'd shared with his nwónnenanna and slept.

While Okpararebisi slept, the Queen spied on her mate. She had introduced him to sweet wine so he wouldn't notice other weefolks in the palace. But it made the King worse. He knew all his maids and his nwónnenanna's wives. Even though one had died at childbirth, the other boldly contended with her. Grief stricken; she sought every Dibia in the hopes of giving the King an heir, and an end to her shame.

There was a maiden at the time called Enyia who had a keen eye on the Omehia, the King of Evóvuotu. Enyia was the only girl offspring of her *de'nnâ*, she had many boy siblings, and they were too poor to get themselves a bride. She was also the most beautiful youngling in Elichei Kingdom. She turned down the merfolks of Mgbe-etó who came to seek her hand in marriage. She wanted a merfolk who would cater for her whole family. One day, a former maid returned with news that most of the maids had run away from the palace because of the queen. She ahd some ideas. She was young, came from a lineage of fertile weefolks, and the queen was old. Thus, she could become the King's weemate, give him an heir, and get enough dowry for her brothers to take a weemate.

She decided to work at the palace as an opportunity to get close enough to marry the king. She knew most of the maidens that left were beautiful, and believed the queen thought them rivals. To gain the approval of the queen, she decided to disguise her beauty. So, when she approached El'ikenueze, she rubbed palm kernel oil on her skin with a special paste from a fungus her nné used in chasing rodents from the house. It wasn't a horrible smell, but it was strong. When she mixed them with the paste of black mushroom her fair skin became dark and patchy, and she oozed of dead fish.

Enyia had always admired Chinwó. Chinwó was the only maid in the palace who didn't cower when the King approached. For that reason, the Queen didn't like her. Chinwó didn't mind. When the Queen doubled her chores, she'd do it. The Queen, angry that she hadn't hurt the young weefolk's feelings, started maltreating her in any possible form.

It was in one of such feats that the King discovered Chinwó. Her strength ensnared him, and her youth made him desire to have her. His weemate and her kin weren't getting any younger and would soon pass babeling-bearing age. He beckoned Chinwó to come to his hut, but she always meandered an escape from that duty. The more she resisted, the more Omehia, the King desired her and decided he would make her submit to being his weemate. Omehia was curious to find out how Chinwó got her confidence if only to boast before his chiefs in this trying time of his reign. He became more observant. So observant that he noticed that every fortnight Chinwó would go to the bath-hut much later than usual and still return smelling of her chores. Suspecting that she had a lover nearby, he decided to follow her.

Enyia saw the King follow Chinwó, thinking Chinwó was going to meet her lover, as this was prohibited in the palace, she tried to give Chinwó a signal. Chinwó wasn't watching so she cut through the bath-hut and tossed a stone at Chinwó and slanted her head in the direction of the King.

61

Her nné saw Chinwó change direction and swiftly left suspecting that her offspring had given her up.

Chinwó snuck back to the bath-hut, but Omehia was standing in front of it. She gave herself to him because he was eyeing her suspiciously, and she didn't want to be beheaded or hung on a pike.

Enyia detested Chinwó for giving in, but they became friends after that incident much because Enyia wanted to make sure that Chinwó wouldn't stand in the way of her becoming queen.

Soon after Okpararebisi moved into the hut, he discovered Omehia's desire for an heir. He also became aware of his insatiable desire for Uzò. But he wanted nothing to do with her. So, whenever he felt the stirrings in his loin, he disguised himself as Omehia and visited the weefolks in the palace. He soon began to detest the weefolks in the palace because Omehia had access to them and step out of its bounds.

The Queen became desperate after she overheard her husband ask for Chinwó's hand in marriage. She went to a seer who prepared herbs for her. Chinwó and Enyia had already eaten from the leftovers of a hunter's gift to the king. To avoid punishment, they hid the food the Queen gave them. All that ate that night, male and female, became sterile.

As the sun rose, Enyia knew she didn't have time on her hands, especially after Chinwó informed her that the King had asked for her hand in marriage. The Queen had fallen ill, and Enyia couldn't escort her friend home to bring her people for the marriage rites. The herbalist came to see the Queen and gave her some herbs. No one was to see the Queen and the Queen was not to leave her hut for a few moons. As the queen was on a curfew, the maids were sent off to their families.

Enyia, seeing the opportunity she'd hoped for, cleaned herself. As soon as darkness began to fade, she went to visit the palm wine tapper to get fresh wine. Knowing a few herbs, courtesy of her late nné, she applied some on her body, some she added to her cooking. She equally added a special one to the keg of palm wine then waited on the King as was customary - the Queen had banned this.

Omehia ogled her, but she pretended not to notice. A few minutes after he'd eaten, he urged her to come to him. She did, but when he tried to hold her, she withdrew.

"What can I offer this damsel to urge her to welcome me?"

"Your heart, your Majesty!" Enyia curtsied as she said it. Her heart beat wildly within her as she prayed her cousin had sent the message to the King's counsel. She offered him more wine, which he took and hurriedly gulped.

Omehia chuckled. "You can't have that. Ask for something else."

She curtsied but said nothing.

"Bold and stubborn. I have a weemate, and I have promised another," Omehia paused and pondered. "Custom demands that I pay your bride price to make you mine, and you know I'm only allowed two weemates."

Enyia curtsied again but said nothing.

Omehia was now restless and shook his legs to distract himself. The maidens that visited his hut in the cloak of darkness had been ordered to visit their parents. Defeated, he decided to make a false promise. "You will have the privileges of a Queen in this palace."

"The King has spoken," the Prime Minister spoke. He and the rest of the elders curtsied.

"So shall it be!" the rest of the council members said. A

few elders nodded their approval.

"My King," the Prime Minister started when the rest of the council sat down. "Why didn't you make her your weemate?"

"I promised another," Omehia retorted through clenched teeth. Annoyed that they'd invited themselves yet again. He gestured at one of his guards. They had an exchange, and then he sent him away. Omehia rose, unable to bear being polite and tolerant anymore, he shielded his appendage and pulled Enyia with him into his hut.

That night Enyia moved into Nwóna'azu's hut. That's how Enyia became the first concubine in the history of Evóvuotu.

Rumours began to spread that the King was defiling the weefolks of El'ikenueze. On two occasions, while a weefolk was being defiled, the King was with Chinwó. Discovering this, they began to suspect it was a youth. More so, the King walked with a limp because one of his legs was shorter than the other.

The Queen was sure it was her husband behind the atrocities. So, when she heard her name used in music announcing her shame, she stabbed him to death. They loved her and didn't have the courage to behead her, so they hung her in the evil forest instead.

Okpararebisi woke up and realised he'd been asleep for a whole season due to exhaustion. It aggrieved him that in that time, Omehia had introduced the idea of having a concubine, and married Chinwó. he had hoped to take Chinwó as his weemate if he failed to find Chinasa. He decided he wasn't going to wait any longer, especially as the scandal didn't take as much effect as he'd hoped. He watched the procession of the queen to the evil forest and waited.

At sundown, he went to Oche-Eze, the Chief Priest who immediately summoned the elders. By the third Moon Okpararebisi was coronated. He didn't marry. He had inherited his de'nnâ's nwónnenanna, Cheta's weemate; Omehia's weemate, Chinwó; and concubine, Enyia. He continued searching for Chinasa while he maintained his search for Ahu, the Prime Minister that stole the love of his life.

The past ten cycles had been heady. He'd become more wanton with his approach to having an heir to the throne. Yet, no maiden had conceived for him, not even the weemates he'd taken advantage of. He started to suspect that the weefolks weren't the problem, but he couldn't accept defeat. He had Ófòr-Nkigwe and Ófòr-Oguneli and thus couldn't be the problem.

He terrorised weefolks, trampled on merfolks, and turned their younglings into slaves. Not openly at first, but then hunger thrived. It seeped into the rest of Evóvuotu, and that became a weapon in his hands too. Merfolks sold their younglings to him in exchange for food. Some gave him their offsprings like one would share his food. He, in turn, shared the maidens amongst some of his elders to keep them quiet. Soon he had parcels of lands in every hamlet of Evóvuotu.

In the first and only uprising, half of his farm produce and the yams in his barn were taken. He decided to bury the pearls of Oko River so that no one could use magic against him, or on his belongings. It also made it easy for him to sense where trouble was brewing, but only within the palace kingdom.

He nipped all uprisings. He was never able to see ahead because, when he did, a part of his body would go limp and stop working entirely. He couldn't heal himself. Instead, he used herbs and, since it was caused by magic it took a really long time to heal.

For the next twenty cycles of seasons, he desired to extend his lifespan. He had an innate feeling that only his soulmate would give him all he desired. He had vowed to make Chinasa his. He believed his offsprings would come from her. If he could find a way to extend his lifespan, then he would have enough time to find her. He wanted an heir. He needed her.

He sighed ruefully leaving his thoughts. Now he was weak he couldn't prevent any harm from coming to him. The gods had ensured that he didn't have a legitimate childling. He'd been sure that he had childlings out there from his time with Uzò but couldn't find them even with the sight.

The moon gave way for the sun, and neither Uzò nor Anyaeze returned. He decided to give them two moons to decide before using force. He detested the fact that he had to grovel to her. Yet, he was suspicious of her cloaking their boy childling for so long.

9.

In the interim, near the edge of Akanônu farmlands, in the Mekwele clan, a wedding was being held. A wedding between Erinma and a man from a distant Kingdom called Ité. Bachanna, the leader of the age-grade of El'ikenueze was almost drunk. He drank to extinguish his anguish. He had done everything possible to woo the bride, but she had chosen Ité. He didn't believe in love at first sight, but after discovering that Ezinma had only met Ité once before his people brought wine and gifts, the idea nagged at his resolve.

He sniggered at himself and burped sluggishly as he watched the proceedings. Ezinma, the most kind-hearted living folk he knew, was slipping off his hands, and he was getting drunk. There was nothing he could do. She had chosen. He had to respect that even though it made him what to strangle the usurper. He just needed them to get it over and done with. He could have faked an illness if he wasn't there to represent his de'nnâ. His thought, his hope and dream had revolved around her and now it revolved around his head strangling any subsiding sorrow. The wedding was barely over when the town crier announced that the King demanded the presence of the merfolks in their twenty-fifth cycle and older. Before the present King, no town crier had ever announced an impromptu meeting. More so, it was usually when the sun was setting or, in the cases of an emergency, before the sun rose. The merfolks within the age-group grumbled all the way to the palace, Ité in tow because the King had made no exceptions.

Ezinma, deciding to surprise Ité by going ahead of him. She was supposed to await his return, but she was worried that he might be waylaid by the bullies who attacked him the day before their wedding. They'd done this because she didn't marry a merfolk from their clan. Her nné had insisted that she should not leave until Ité returned, but she had run out of patience. She also carried a basket of leftovers from the wedding. Her excitement numbed her exhaustion. She knew no harm would come to her if she took the path that led to the stream and avoided the main road.

Thirsty, she branched to the stream. She heard voices. Assuming that it would be her cousins and their friends as they'd made the large tree that sectioned the roads to the stream their hangout, she ignored it. She never understood the amusement of hanging down from trees. It was only when she got to the mouth of the stream that she realised who it was. Her attempted escape was too late; the King had seen her.

He never walks in these paths, she thought. *It was for peasants like herself. Besides he is supposed to be in a meeting with the age-group he'd summoned.* Ezinma ran and called for help. (If only she'd known why her parents had been so protective - no one came when they heard a girl childling or youngling scream, they simply changed direction.)

The King ordered his guards to take her to the palace. She fought them with all her might. As they got close to the compound, she turned and in the twisting of her body, broke her neck. Her death was instantaneous, and this angered the King so much that he made the guards carrying her leprous.

The meeting finally came to an end with the return of the King. He gave his blessings and left them feeling as gloomy as he was. He had increased tax for every merfolk within the age-group he'd summoned. He also demanded a tenth of everything they harvested. Ité wasn't hungry or interested, he wanted to take his weemate home but stayed for refreshment as custom demanded.

On their way out, a commotion ensued. Some guards tried to cordon off the leprous guards. A path was created to let the King's guests pass. One of these guests caught sight of something on the ground and tapped on the shoulder of the person ahead of him, then pointed to their left. They nodded at each other smiling because it was covered with the hides of the royal family. Curiously, they moved their line closer to the item. The one that tapped his friend's shoulder used his feet to brush the large hide off the bamboo stretcher, and a hand fell out. Alarmed, he jumped back with a shriek. His shriek attracted the attention of others nearby. They couldn't get a word out of him because he jerked violently as he pointed. The guards quickly cut through the crowd to cordon the place, but the eager group intercepted them.

Ité, eager to get to his bride, was oblivious of the second commotion. It was only when one of them shouted his weemate's name that he stopped in his tracks. Her name being mentioned a few more times made him want to confront the merfolk. He menacingly shoved his way to the centre of the gathering and fell on his knees. He tried not to cry as he observed. His Ezinma's eyes were red and swollen as if she'd been crying; her head lolled, one hand was curled into a fist, and the other hand lay open like she was pleading. It was his wedding day, a day he was supposed to take his weemate home, but they had to have an accursed age-group meeting. He stretched his hand and closed her eyes, muttering curses.

Whatever he said, the merfolks rhythmically stamped their feet in agreement. They later dragged him away from the body. Someone else helped him carry the body of his lifeless weemate – it was Bachanna. The guards tried to prevent them but realising they were outnumbered, stalled.

That same day, in Avaliland, a youngling called Omezie made her way into El'ikenueze against the advice of her nwónnénné. She knew a shortcut through Nowele that would take her to the edge of El'ikenueze before the farmers left their homes. No living folk could go through Nowele except her, her nwónnénné and some others who are no longer living folks. She was the White Priestess.

It came to be that sixteen cycles of seasons ago, a child was born to Amauche and Azu of Emeka-Obi's clan in Akpunwó. On the eve of her birth, three spotless chicks strayed into the compound. The pair who been barren for a very long time named the babeling, Omezie. So that on Omezie's eight cycle, she was whisked off to her nwónnénné's compound in the hills that shielded Agbalanya Forest to be prepared in the rites of becoming the White Priestess. She was to remain within her nwónnénné's compound until the rites where completed. So, on her thirteenth cycle, she was paraded around the entire Kingdom on completion of the first of three rites. Three cycles later, on the eve of the second rite, her nwónnénné went into a trance that lasted two seasons. No one knew what to do as it had never happened, and even though Omezie had been taught how to go into such a trance she wasn't permitted to. Even if she did, she wouldn't know where and how to find her nwónnénné. As her nwónnénné was supposed to announce the commencement of the next rite, it couldn't be held.

When her nwónnénné finally came through, she was struck with an unusual sickness. Whenever she asked her nwónnénné to treat it, her nwónnénné would smile. Omezie knew it was bad because her nwónnénné naturally kept nothing from her. Also, there was always a lasting look of worry in her nwónnénné's eye. More so, she wasn't allowed

70

out of her nwónnénné's sight. She was banned from going outside the hut. A mason who owed her nwónnénné several favours built a bath-hut in one corner of the hut so Omezie wouldn't have an excuse to leave her hut. Water was brought to her and she was taught a weaving spell to heat it. Frustrated, she confined her thoughts to the day she would finally be free from her nwónnénné. Her nné and her de'nnâ had come to visit her once when they'd finished their tour of the twelve Kingdoms a cycle ago. Her nné had told her that they weren't supposed to when she asked her nwónnénné was cross.

The beginning of a new season increased her eagerness and yearning. She stopped concentrating, distracted by her hopes and desires. On one such occasion, she didn't hear her nwónnénné announce that she was going to get herbs from the Agbalanya forest. Her nwónnénné's compound had direct access to it as it started at the back of their food-hut, and their house was at the edge of the forest. Her nwónnénné had gone in search of a specific herb to ease the labour of a pregnant weefolk in the treatment hut and returned limping.

When Omezie asked about it, she was given

a stern glare. She never brought it up again. The following day, before the cock crew, her nwónnénné came into her hut and waited patiently until she woke up. Her nwónnénné was anything but patient. It was also a discomfort for Omezie who had never been underdressed in front of her aunt. When she was clean, dressed and fed, her nwónnénné cleared her throat and paused dramatically then said.

"Night has come upon us. I have shielded the evil arrow that threatens our kind, but I'm afraid it will not be enough. You need to leave for Enwere right away. I have packed for you."

Her nwónnénné gestured to the leather bag beside her, a special bag that she never parted with. She raised a brow at her nwónnénné who seemed calm and was startled when her nwónnénné gripped her tightly as she sternly added.

"Do not turn back. Remember, you are our future, and I have taught you everything I know. Kneel, let me bless you."

Several questions passed through Omezie's mind, more so, when her nwónnénné's voice carried a desperate plea.

"But the blessing is after..."

"Kneel!" Her nwónnénné ordered then placed a curved pendant with a jagged stone as clear as water in a leather string over Omezie's neck. "Henceforth, you shall be called Anyanazuvuanyamgbede. Hope is despairing, but not while you're safe. Go through Agbalanya, help will meet you there." Her nwónnénné sighed and began to bring and replace items in the bag to Omezie's despair. "Where they take you is a message to the Keeper of Rimeóku, he doesn't like it when living folks keep him waiting. This is a gift for Ene-e, when it's time he'll take you to a safe place."

Suspicious, Omezie frowned and waited for an opportunity to voice her concern. It didn't come.

"Sorrow and joy, dark and light, moon and sun."

"Watch for the pawn of darkness for its lure is strong,

and its lust is true. Like life in the blood is its fire. Shred your heart from its grasp. For a merfolk can find his way back but not you, my dear."

Omezie decided to bite her tongue. This was the opportunity she had been longing for, but she saw tears stream down her nwónnénné's face and frowned. Her nwónnénné handed her a whirly tusk with gold engravings. Sighing, she brought out a folded hide. The hide had an unusual glow; the raffia it was lined with was the colour of the inside of a living folk's palm, its edges was tweaked with a different kind of raffia that couldn't be seen with the naked eye and gold strings was woven into it. The gold strings looked like they were moving. and then she placed a hand on Omezie's shoulder then quickly pulled her in a hug and shoved her off before turning away from her.

"Be wise and practice all I've taught you. Now go! For you must leave at once!"

She couldn't tell her nwónnénné that she had received a message in her dreams for the King of All Living Folks because she would have cast it off as nothing just like she had been doing for the past four cycles. Omezie hurriedly left the hut heading towards the path her nwónnénné had once taken her.

But her heart was heavy, and anger began to seep into it as she questioned her nwónnénné in her mind.

I'm now the Priestess of Light! If I could be crowned before the rite was completed, why then was I separated from my family? Why should I have hidden here like someone infested with leprosy?

Omezie peered outside the hut, trying to curb her excitement at the same time as trying to adjust to the brightness. The sun had only just risen, so she had enough time to go into town and return to Agbalanya's Forest. She would still make it back in time to meet the Enwere. She had never met them before, but her aunt had once told her that they didn't come out at night because they didn't need to. Since she had a journey of three moons, she might as well get some food from her nné. Thinking of her nné's cooking made her mouth water. She licked her lips and focused on the dreams she'd had about the King of All Living Folks, then organised them according to their theme as she made her way into the palace Kingdom.

Absentmindedly, she made her way to the palace. Unknown to her, there was an unusual treaty, and no one knew why it was made that way. It just was so. The treaty was that the White Priestess was never to leave her compound without forewarning or death will visit their kind like a plague.

What's more? A White Priestess was to have no vain motive.

10.

As soon as Omezie, now Anyanazuvuanyamgbede, the White Priestess got to the boundaries of the El'ikenueze, the Palace Kingdom. She pulled her hide-raffia-gold cloak over her head. She knew where to find the palace; with the herald of Òfòr-Nkigwe gave him away. She entered the hut stealthily and tapped on the King's shoulder. He turned, not seeing her: the cloak made her invisible to everyone. He finally saw her when he tapped into the power of the Òfòr-Oguneli.

She curtsied.

Okpararebisi gasped on seeing her. She was the most beautiful weefolk he had ever laid his eyes on. He got up and approached her with a leer in his eyes.

Okpararebisi approached her like a hunter inspecting its

74

prey as he appraised her.

Omezie blinked and frowned. She had heard a rumour when she was a childling that the priestess exuded a scent that lured merfolks. They had no control over their actions, and the only way to stop them was in their death. The way he gazed at her made her wonder if there was truth to that story. He seemed fixated on her, and she felt like something was crawling down her spine. She had forgotten that he had all the powers of the Ófòr-Oguneli at his disposal. She had even forgotten why she'd ventured into the palace. She turned to run but was frozen on the spot. Now apprehensive about her nwónnénné, she couldn't even remember any weavings that would protect her; her mind had gone blank, even if it hadn't, she had not been paying attention.

He smiled impudently as he made his way towards her. The door latched at the wave of his finger. He clicked his fingers, and the bushels came on like they had been struck with the spark of a flint. He beckoned her. She obeyed; her limbs were no longer in her control. He flicked his finger continuously, but nothing happened. He stretched his hand to pull the dress off her body, but as he tried to tear the dress, it glistened brightly searing his palms. Agitated, he tried again. Again. And once more.

Omezie looked down at her dress in surprise then smiled in triumph just as a sharp pain pierced through her side, and she saw a vision of her aunt falling and the maids clutching at their chests. She gasped and looked around surreptitiously for a way out. She prayed, hoped that the stories weren't true. But she knew. It was much more than a dream.

Okpararebisi was grinning, but his grin looked frozen. His eyes were starry as he carried the fire towards her.

She comported herself to look defiant. Then she remembered why she had come. She opened her mouth, but words weren't coming out. She blinked and tried again. No word came out. She tried to raise her hands to defend herself, but they didn't respond to her. They were now his to compel, and she still couldn't remember the spell to shield herself from harm.

Okpararebisi flinched and became more determined to get her out of the hide. He tried scorching it, but it remained the same. He sat on the bed near her and pondered on the way to remove the garment. It was a thick barrier. He could get to her but couldn't get past the dress. Smiling, he motioned for her to face him, and she did. He rubbed his hands eagerly and motioned for her to pull up the dress, and she did.

She whimpered as she did, but he was oblivious to it.

He gestured, and she walked to the bed. He got up and perused her like she was something he was trying to fathom then he joined her and wiped the tears from her eyes tenderly, dreamily.

If Omezie pleaded, he was oblivious to it.

He waved his hand, and she parted her legs.

Tears streamed down her temples, and she closed her eyes, overwhelmed with a sense of foreboding. *Was this what my aunt meant? What will I say to her now?*

Okpararebisi paused, then tilted his head to listen. Someone was in his court. He could feel it. He let his mind sail around the palace until it got his court, his body stiffened when he found out it was Uzò. He quickly retreated to his body and left, making sure to latch the door. Feeling lightheaded, he reprimanded himself; he'd forgotten why he'd stopped mind-travelling.

Uzò's back was turned to him as she glanced around his court. He gritted his teeth stunned by his desire for her, a stirring he thought he'd gotten over. He wondered how she managed to get in without rousing his guards. He watched her for a while then cleared his throat noisily. Uzò turned around slowly. He smiled nervously, but she didn't smile back. There seemed to be a wall between them because each time he neared her, he felt something shove him away.

She wanted to introduce him to his offspring, she murmured.

Okpararebisi laughed. It couldn't be. He had his suspicions, but he didn't believe her. He raised doubtful brows at the merfolk that walked in after him, was no less than forty cycles.

"Whose did you say he was?" he whispered, still trying to figure out what the barrier between them was. It reminded him of the woman and her daughter in the woods. The same push. It was his spell. He should have known.

Uzò let out a long mirthless laugh.

It reminded him of the time he'd spent in her hut, and he sank on the throne as his legs could no longer carry him. He was doleful for just a few seconds; remembering that she'd told him their childling was dead. He thought of strangling her, but she had a hold on him that he couldn't yet fathom. He would have loved to know how she managed to keep him out of sight for so long.

Okpararebisi turned his back to them as he smiled his satisfaction. His heir was home. He just needed to find a way to make the Kingdom accept his offspring as the crown prince so he could become King when the time came.

"What is his name?"

"Ask him," Uzò responded and gestured to the merfolk beside her.

"Anyaeze, it is," the merfolk sniggered and added in a condescending tone. "You're not my de'nnâ."

Okpararebisi shrugged nonchallantly and retorted. "Yes, you're a seed of my loin. A merfolk who cannot live under my roof but a seed of my loin none the less."

Anyaeze looked at his nné, she nodded and he sighed despairingly. "You are a grandfather. I ask that you pass the totem capes to my offspring. I want nothing from you, but it would be unfair of me to deprive my offspring of that right."

"But..."

"This is his foreskin, so you don't need to set your eyes on him," Uzò said and sauntered out of the room, pulling her offspring with her.

Okpararebisi smiled meditatively. He wouldn't disappoint even though he knew a ceremony was required to pass on the totem cape. He wanted to ask why his offspring was expecting two totem capes but being that it wasn't a priority to concern himself with, he ignored it altogether. He picked up the foreskin and tried to sniff the childling's sprit to follow its scent and began to sneeze. It was covered in pepper. He chuckled limply.

Uzò was a spitfire, he missed that about her. He shook his head. Just seeing her undid him. But he wasn't going to let her get away with placing him under a spell, and neither could she keep him from his newly discovered lineage. He blew a gentle breeze into the foreskin, and everything she had imbued in it wafted away. What he didn't know was that she had covered the foreskin with pepper so he wouldn't realise that there were two foreskins because he had two offshoots from Anyaeze. Oblivious, he sniffed the foreskin again and followed its trail. It led him to Chinwó's hut. Then realisation set in; the silhouette with a lamp all those seasons ago was Chinwó, and her nné was Uzó. He bit the inside of his cheek. He should have noticed; her insolence during his uncle's reign and her insubordinations in his time. Uzò must have cast a spell on Chinwó so he could find her repulsive and that wasn't the case before he ascended the throne.

He made a mental note to undo that spell if only to hurt

Uzó.

He searched for a babeling. He found a childling instead. He had over the seasons mastered how to summon someone with his mind and hoped that the childling didn't have a strong sprit. He told the childling to come to his hut as soon as everyone else was asleep. It didn't work. Then in passing, he heard Uzò call the childling, Ogbuogu, then summoned the childling by its name.

Omezie, the Anyanazuvuanyamgbede got up and walked out of the room as soon as Okpararebisi left. She had succeeded in eluding some of the guards, but she needed enough cover to escape unnoticed. She waited patiently for the cloud to cover the moon. If she ever got out of the compound in one piece, she would never be disobedient. She was about to come out of her hiding spot when she heard light footsteps approaching. She crouched lower, but the footsteps continued towards her.

Seeing that it was a childling, she knelt and pleaded with the childling. But it laughed. It had just come out of the large hut Okpararebisi had entered when he left her. In a few seconds, Okpararebisi was standing beside the childling. He'd used the childling as bait.

He murmured proudly and tapped the childling's shoulder. "Ogbuogu."

Ogbuogu nodded and walked back in the direction he came from.

Okpararebisi grinned sheepishly. "I may be old, my dear, but I have experience on my side. Now come with me!"

It hurt to resist, but she did for several minutes. He pulled her to his room. She slanted her head and saw a few weefolks in the distance and called to them for help. None of them came.

He shook his head, muttering, "Why bother?"

She continued to cry, scream and resist. He spun and drew a line around her neck with his finger so no sound would come out. As she trudged behind him, no longer in control of her limbs, she heard hurried footsteps and the weefolks in the distance were gone.

Defeated, all she could do was cry.

11.

As soon as Okpararebisi got off her, Omezie summoned all the strength she could muster to prevent herself from crying. She closed her eyes and saw a vision of her aunt crossing Mini-Echiche and anger welled in her. She felt it crawl and swim within her in the rapid speed of the rising tides. She licked her lips, welcoming it.

There's no going back now, no turning back the hand of time and no chance getting forgiveness.

She was doomed and was ready to take everyone with

her. She got up and ran out of the room and had almost reached the gate when she saw the other weefolks. Oblivious to the fact that the sun had risen, or that she was naked, but distracted by the unnerving pull of several nimbuses, she spun, tilting her head so and so.

A viewers were muttering and exclaiming, which attracted the attention of others within the compound. The childlings who had gathered around a few peacocks with sticks and stones were now focused on her. An elderly weefolk shooed the childlings and younglings away, but no one tried to help her though they looked on, shaking their heads.

Her eyes darkened when she saw Ogbuogu. She was still trying to shake off the pull of the nimbuses when a glint caught her eye. Glancing sideways, she discovered that it was the Ófòr-Oguneli. She walked purposefully towards it; and the guards who tried to intercept her approach, she cast aside with the wave of her hand. The nimbus of the White Priestess within her threatened to overwhelm her as she moved closer to the Ófòr-Oguneli, but she suppressed it. There was rumbling like an approaching storm which only lasted a few seconds when she got to close to it.

Okpararebisi saw where she was heading and materialised by the door. Sensing his approach, she quickly grabbed the Ófòr-Oguneli. Okpararebisi folded his arms, leaned on the wall at the entrance of his court, and watched; amused and finding her resilient determination irresistible. The glint of anger in Omezie's eyes aroused him it seemed to increase the glow in her which dulled his drab fragility. More so, she was the first weefolk he longed for since Uzò and Chinasa.

This one I can keep, he thought as he began to walk towards her.

"Don't you dare!" Omezie murmured, her voice was

81

barely audible, and her lips were trembling.

"What did you think would happen when you held it? How does it feel to be near such power and be unable to wield it?" He asked with a smug look on his face and paused.

She let out a ragged sigh as she wadded through the protective shield of the Ófòr-Oguneli.

Oblivious of what she'd done, he nodded coyly. "A merfolk of my potential can make you a great weefolk. With you by my side, all folks will adore me, you even. Why then do you stand against my heart's desire?"

The anger in her was so intense that her short brown hair rapidly grew long, wavy and glossy black, and her eyes no longer red. She let out a guttural sound then laughed. Her laughter quickly turned to a mournful cackle then she screeched. It was so simple and unassuming, but everyone within the palace walls screamed in pain as blood seeped out of their ears.

He winced at the sound of screaming but continued walking towards her and stopped when Ogbuogu called him. He turned to see that almost everyone in the compound was in his court pleading his help. Not wanting to lose integrity before them, he lunged forward to take the Ófòr-Oguneli from her, but each time he caught her, she rippled and disappeared. It was by the fourth time that he realised there were all illusions of her. He decided to undo the illusion, but to do that, he had to cancel his own too as it came from the same source; the Ófòr-Oguneli.

She had just seen a vision of her nwónnénné sailing through Mini-Echiche. Omezie had turned fleetingly into an angry and mad weefolk. Her cackle grew louder and shriller.

Okpararebisi looked up at her, startled, worried, and suspicious. He hurried toward her and raised a hand to slap her. But she tilted her head and sent him flying across the room without touching him. It was then that he recognised the power in her, but it wasn't supposed to exist. When he'd first seen her, he suspected it was the scorch-proof hide she wore and then the distracting glow pushing through from within her. He'd been taught the allusions of every power except the one standing in front of him. He'd learned of every power, stones, seasons in his search for immortality.

Is she the forbidden one? Is her glow the secret to immortality?

Omezie's eyes danced around wildly as she spoke in an eerie voice. "I called for help, but my weefolks looked on." She appeared in various places as she continued. "Your childlings and your younglings stared at my nakedness. Your boy-childling shall hunger for this and will not find it in any girl-childling, dead or alive. O girl offsprings, your boy offsprings shall graze your bed like the bulls of Rigene Forest. Feast your eyes! Feast your eyes! Feast your eyes for your de'nnâ's sin has come upon you!"

Snickering, he muttered, "My sins cannot be visited on the seed of my loins. It's not the law of nature." Okpararebisi grimaced as he struggled to pick himself up.

83

Omezie scoffed gleefully. "Gone are the days when merfolks fell by their sins. You all chose your fate the day you shut your mouth to my pleas and those of the numerous weefolks who've been brought in here against their will. The oppressions of the people who stare at you. Ah, the poor that lingered at your gate for a morsel of garri."

Now quite irritated, he ordered. "Hand me that sceptre!" Okpararebisi ordered.

"It was never yours to begin with." Omezie said and glanced at it, her eyes gleaming with mischief. then whispered to the staff. "Find and protect your wielder for Awele will soon awaken."

She paused, slanted a look at Okpararebisi, then to taunt him, she began to swing it. "You want this, don't you?"

"Hand it over. Now!"

She stopped swinging the Ófòr-Oguneli and tossed it. He stretched his hand to catch it, but less than an inch from his reach she made a fist, and it shattered. She clapped gleefully as the nimbuses wafted out of the pieces of Ófòr-Oguneli.

84

"The White Priestess!" Ginika, Uzò's maidservant, gasped drawing Uzò's attention to the shattered sceptre. It was known that only the White Priestess held such power. Annoyed and aggrieved, Uzò looked on mournfully. She'd done everything to become the White Priestess, she'd even made all likely rivals ill with leprosy. Although Omezie was a curious and obnoxious childling, she had always been too sickly to be considered a rival. Glaring contemptuously at the girl who never had to fight for anything, she saw a dark green nimbus veil of mist escape from a shard of the Ófòr-Oguneli. Not liking it or the others in the same hue, she ignored it. But when, she caught sight of a red nimbus, she chased it. It had flown too high to reach so she shoved one of the weefolks, at the entrance, out of the way to get an orange one. Desperate for more, she chased after them, knocking a few shuddering folks as she chased, and only succeeded in acquiring another in dark purple. As soon as the purple nimbus entered her, the orange one pulled out. Feeling tingly within her and itchy outside, she snuck back into the King's court.

The nimbus veils of mist went out in flight to its next possessor but were inhibited by the pearls of the Oko River with which the Okpararebisi's ancestors had bounded El'ikenueze. The pearls of the Oko River repelled magic. Unable to find their owners, the nimbus veils of mist searched for willing or eager hearts, which was difficult in the height of despair in the kingdom, most of all the nimbus veils of mist didn't recognise motive.

Amongst the beggars at the palace gate, was an old weefolk from Rumuochara Kingdom, who had been a maid most of her early life; the dark green nimbus embraced her, and she got up with a bone-cracking stretch, her hair was no longer white but black with a few specks of grey. The inflammation in her joints were gone. Not wanting to be discovered by the King, she looked around surreptitiously and quickly blended into the crowd. While she was making her way out of El'ikenueze, three more nimbus veils slammed into her almost knocking the air out of her lungs; they were all in shades of green but a much lighter hue than the first. She stumbled into a blind merfolk who regained his sight instantly and went after her.

The sun had reached its peak by the time the first set of people leaving the palace kingdom got to its boundaries. An invisible wall prevented them from getting through. With time, they understood that it was only those imbued with nimbus that couldn't get through. Exhausted and hungry they remained, hoping help would come but the longer they waited, the more they despaired and each time they'd their nimbus would escape and find other hosts.

The old weefolk, no longer looking old, couldn't cross the boundary. Exhausted with finding a way. Not willing to give herself to despair, she walked away from the crowd who couldn't get through and sat down to think. Sighing, she made her way back to the palace.

By sundown, farmers began to make their way out of the Palace Kingdom. Among them were two younglings, when they got near the wall, the younger one stopped abruptly asked, "Nwoneri, do you see that?"

"See what?" the older of the two asked nonchalantly as he passed through the invisible wall.

One of the merfolks, sitting near the wall attempted to follow the youngling, met an invisible wall, and limped back to where he was sitting.

The younger one was startled by what he'd seen and didn't dare wall through the wall. He called out to his sibling, who picked a stone for his catapult but Nwoneri was oblivious to his sibling's plea. The younger youngling continued to call on Nwoneri while he cautiously walked to the wall and closed his eyes to pass through it. He was almost out when all the nimbus veils from the despairing folks entered him, causing him to fall forward, thereby knocking out some of the unsettled nimbus veils.

Nwoneri ran to his sibling's side and felt something sting him as he touched his sibling's face. The youngling belched as he sat up, his subtle belch was so strong it knocked Nwoneri's catapult out of his hand.

Meanwhile, at the palace, there was a pandemonium; some people shuddered as the nimbus veil entered them, those in the palace that the nimbus veils of mist had touched were healed of their broken eardrum. soldiers and maids, alike. Some, sensing the change in them and suspecting the king had done something to them, began to withdraw, carrying what they could slip away with. Ogbuogu felt sick after a nimbus entered him and went outside

In the King's court, most of the weefolks were shouting mundane words. Some gasped and cowered, others knelt pleading for their lives. The childlings and younglings in the court did whatever each of their parents did except for a few curious ones; they simply couldn't hear each other.

Okpararebisi mourned his inability to fix the damage the White Priestess had done. He ran outside hysterically chasing the nimbus veils of mist and caught his escaping servants. Already in a vexed mood, he tapped into the residual power of the Ófòr-Oguneli, clapped his hands and turned them to dust. At the same time, Enyia, a heavily pregnant Chinwó and Chinwó's maid who'd been at the royal waters the whole time, saw the commotion and stealthily snuck into their huts. Not long after that, Chinwó went into labour.

Anyanazuvuanyamgbede closed her eyes, summoning her scorch-proof hide then raised her hands up, so the gold-flaked hide passed through like it was being pulled over her. As soon as the dress sat on her, it began to change. The gold flecks in the raffia flickered, and fire engulfed the dress, causing ripples on the fabric. When the fire stopped, the dress was silky gold, black, red, and long.

She cackled again and declared, "Commit to memory this day. For when you forget the owl will cry. The river-horse will roar. The tamed foxes of the Agbalanya Forest will herald the echoes of Rimeoku. The hummingbird will announce the day of hunting. The eagle will fail to soar. The lion will fail to brag. The vultures will have their fill. Yes, that day is nigh…" she continued chanting.

Uzò, irritated, moved closer to Anyaeze holding a spear and flailing her free hand. As soon as she touched Anyaeze, he tugged the spear off her and tossed it at Omezie. It went through the side of her neck. Blood gushed from her half-open neck as her head lolled backwards. That's how it came to be that Omezie, the Anyanazuvuanyamgbede of Evóvuotu, the White Priestess, the last of her kind died.

Okpararebisi and Ogbuogu walked in simultaneously.

Ogbuogu was drawn to the object that fell from Omezie's hand. It was a charm, an emblem of Omezie's kind. He went to where she was and picked it up. It looked like gnarled claws. Three shiny objects were embedded in each of them. One shone like the sun, another like the moon and another like a rain cloud. They were melded together. Then he looked surreptitiously around, tucked it in his sheathpoc, and went back to stand briefly between Ginika and Uzò before slipping out again.

Okpararebisi saw his chance of immortality on the floor and fell on his knees; she no longer emitted the glow that fascinated him, and she seemed to be declaring her victory because there was a smile on her lifeless face.

Outside, Ene'e the white antelope materialised at the edge of Okpararebisi's court, glistening white like the lilies on the surface of a pond facing the rising sun and was waiting. As soon as the childling stepped outside the King's court, Ene'e swept a gentle breeze toward it. It nudged the childling into a weefolk who was nursing her ear then he scratched the ground with his hoof - and the childling fell asleep.

He created a portal to his sanctuary while untangling the charm from the childling's grip then created a bubble and sent the charm bracelet to his realm and watched the bubble gradually open to drop the charm in the gourd. Closing the portal, he slipped through the crowd, still invisible, and prayed for Omezie's soul. He created an illusion of the Ófòr-Oguneli on the ground. He tried to gather the real one, but it was impossible because of its loyalty to its wielder. He could only carry the carcass, so he tucked them in an Omeneri bottle. He looked around wearily and shook his head mournfully as the nimbuses flew about aimlessly.

Soon after she shimmered and disappeared. He took the rest of her through the portal, but this time he stopped at the boundary that led to his realm. He frowned, unable to shake off the feeling that he'd forgotten something. Sighing, he removed one of the pearls of the Oko River. Soon after that, the merchant path was open and as people got across the boundaries of the palace kingdom, the uninhabited nimbus veils of mist flew off freely to scout for new hosts.

He closed his eyes and tilted his head, and a bubble began to form at the tip of his horns; he lowered his head, and the Omeneri bottle entered the bubble; blinked, and the Omeneri bottle deposited itself near Ónu's second weemate's hut at another edge of the palace Kingdom. He carried Omezie's remains without touching it, the withered leaves on the ground rose to a narrow heap, and she settled gently on it. Offering thanks to Ugwu, he transformed into a man then summoned a leader in Omezie's clan as he could see that they were receiving their people who'd already crossed Mini-Echiche. Not a spirit to be kept waiting, he summoned one of Omezie's ancestors.

"What is it?" an annoyed wrinkly old merfolk asked as he materialised.

"I bring you one of yours."

The wrinkly old merfolk looked on and shook his head slowly, "She isn't."

"Emeka Obi, you're her first de'nnâ."

"The minute she disobeyed a cardinal rule, she ceased to be one of mine."

"She remains one of yours," Ene'e debated.

The wrinkly old merfolk winced and sniggered. He slowly sat on a seat made of eroding rock covered with moss even though there was no water in the area.

Ene'e solemnly watched the merfolk for a while then said; "Can you unwind the stream? Can you prevent the crickets from chirping? Or can you put a babeling back into its nné's womb? She is the last of her kind, the last of your kindred for a reason."

The wrinkly old merfolk let out a definitive sigh; disappearing, he crooned, "It's been decided."

Frustrated and sensing Ónwu, he frowned. Resigned, he sternly said; "You can stop hiding now." Ene'e slanted his head so he could keep an eye on the damping-illusion he'd created around the Ófòr-Oguneli then moved away to ensure Ónwu wouldn't get close enough to inspect or suspect.

Ónwu, who'd been hovering, harrumphed and turned around to face him, removing his mask of invisibility.

"What do you want?"

90

Ónwu gritted his yellow, decayed teeth. "The soul you stole from me."

"What?"

"Do not act dumb!" Ónwu's eyes glistened bright red, he closed his hands, making his fingernails stand out like a bird's tail then gestured. "I don't like you, and you don't like me, understandably. But you are interfering," Ónwu paused, theatrically rubbed his chin with his knuckle and sighed, "it is quite irritating."

Ene'e scoffed. "Awele will decide that. Until then, stay out of my business."

Ónwu shuddered at the mention of Awele and gulped. "Very well, but this is not over."

"You should find your de'nnâ, you know? You should indeed focus on that."

Disappearing, Ónwu sneeringly glared at him.

Relieved, Ene'e sighed and stared at Omezie's corpse.

Elsewhere. At the boundary that separated El'ikenueze from Elidikenónu, Ité stood over his weemate's grave in her de'nnâ's compound. (Because she didn't have a childling, she had to be buried in her de'nnâ's compound as was his tradition. Her family didn't object because she didn't officially leave the compound with her husband's people, and they wanted their offspring to be buried in peace.) He'd been standing by her grave since sunset, reminiscing on their arduous path to marriage and sighed ruefully. It had gotten so bad, that she once told him it wasn't meant to be, but he was a fighter.

His weemate's parents were worried that he'd died of hunger as he'd been by the grave for over two moons, so they decided to go and carry his body. When they got close, they found him sitting there. When he pulled out a flint, the bride's nné made to stop him, but her husband restrained her.

Ité held the naked flint tightly and pulled it with the other hand. Blood started dripping from his closed fist. He dropped the flint and wiped his eyes, inhaled deeply and murmured; "Blood is life, and life is blood. A curse on him who made you a victim of his tyranny and his generation to come. Death will not give up on his compound. Over his roof, the circling vulture will never lack." He sighed and added. "in his next life, he shall be that which he despised the most."

"Forgiveness will come…" his merfolk-in-law started.

His weefolk-in-law wiped her tears and held her offspring's mermate's hand. "Blessed to a nné 's sacrifice, an offspring's grief, a warrior's fate…" she stumbled and began to sob.

Her mermate wrapped his arms around her, shaking his head. He always believed in forgiveness just like his offspring, the only seed of his loin. "The compass of love will find you, but inherit it you will not, until you find the virtues of pure goodness."

"So be it!" They chorused.

Ité cried along with them because that is what is weemate would have wanted.

12.

In the skies, in the temple of the King of all Imperials, Living and Dead Folks was Awele. Awele the Avenger stood like an imposing statue, tall and regal when he was asleep, which he usually was. Unless he was awake, then he walked with wobbly feet. To the Imperials, he was always better off asleep because when he was awake, he was nosy, vile, mischievous, and daunting.

It wasn't a bad thing usually, except his mates were up to no good which they often were, most of the time. He had become too intrusive, and his colleagues were tired of his springing upon them that they decided to grind the bark of the tanning moon tree.

Awele took pride in Akanchi, his scale of justice and sins

93

and held it up anywhere he went. Although it had an unmeasurable weigh, to Awele, it weighed no more than a leaf. The cries of broken hearts had reached the skies and shook the foundations of the Imperial Kingdom so much so that the brimming Akanchi became overweight and fell pulling Awele with it. Only then did Awele wake up from his slumber.

Awele was so angry to find out what his colleagues had done that he demanded they be made labourers. Since they had left their powers to reside in one delirious tyrant without intervening. He was so angry and so hungry that he decided to quench his thirst with a little more wine, but Oju-Mmanya, the god of mirth and festivity had been bribed with a beautiful wench, so the wine was drugged in exchange for his escapades to be kept away from his weemate.

Half asleep, Awele heard Ité's prayer, and tears spilled out of his closed eyes. He opened his eyes slightly and produced a yellow granule from his waistband and spat in it - the tiny grain in his hand was the size of a merfolk in Evóvuotu. With an unsteady hand, he blew into it but missed Okpararebisi's compound by a journey of two moons. It had landed on an untilled land, in the jagged hills, on the side-of-the-setting-sun of El'ikenueze.

If it was possible to have mood swings in your dream, then this was an epitome of one. As he sailed away in irresistible slumber, he willed an answer to Ité's prayer. But Nwaneri the messenger, undone by gluttony as he paid attention only to the sumptuous buffet ahead of him ordained Omezie's prayer too. Realising what he had done he decided to visit the world of living folks as he would need the Ófòr-Oguneli to change what he had done.

Nwaneri tried to rouse himself and slumped back into the ample vine bench. His stomach was so full that it shone with a smoothness of a babeling's bottom. He resolved to wait a few more hours until the food in his stomach had condensed.

13.

On the third moon since their arrival in Ónu's compound and while Eriri slept, an eerie tune played outside. Ómalichanwa listened. Something about it made the hair on her skin stand. It was hard to resist its pull. She has had the virtue of always following her instinct and the pull felt like a nudge rather than a shove. The problem was, her instinct gave nothing. Refusing to sleep, she stared at the thatched roof.

A light and airy voice spoke through the music. "I have been on a long journey. Can a wanderer find rest in your hands? Can a wanderer find solace in the kindness of your heart? If you can't I'll sing louder. I have wandered, roamed, strayed, roved, tramped and moored. I have swum the ages. From dusk until dawn, from sunrise to sunset, sunup to sundown, moons to sunshines, for cycles of seasons, in search of one such as you. Can you hear my plea? I pray you! Can I find solace in your bosom? I beseech you, hear the plea of a forlorn one."

Ómalichanwa craned her neck and whispered; "Who are you?"

"It is I, the beauty of evolution."

Ómalichanwa slunk back in confusion.

"The metre of experience and the winding path between the sun and the moon, life, and death."

She paused for a while then asked; "What is your name?"

There was no answer. The night was quiet again except for the chirping crickets and croaking frogs but the chirping and croaking were different. It seemed like they were taking

95

turns in sustaining the eerie music. A few minutes later, the eerie tune played again, and then the voice spoke; she asked the same questions, but there was no answer. While she waited, she fell asleep, and then the music started once more. This time it was loud but airy, and the foundation of her uncle's hut shook. She looked at her de'nnâ, but he seemed unperturbed by the tremors.

Then the voice spoke. "O offspring of Eriri, offspring of Chijile of Ichie's line of the royal family of El'ikenueze. I have crossed miles to reach you. Words cannot describe your wisdom nor silence your power. A desperate one beseeches. Will you not hear its plea? You hold fast to your ideals, but you are gentle and generous. Lend me your heart, that I may find solace. Lend me your sight, that I may concede to the beauty I once beheld. Lend me your hand, that I indeed may find my kindred."

"Who are you?"

"I am yours to command, yours to wield, yours to guide and yours to ordain."

Ómalichanwa rolled her eyes.

"I'm the one to whom a babeling's first exclamation is sublime, the one the grave can't hinder in due season. I am the Witness, to enmity, oath, pain, love. To whom seasons lay their ploy for an arbitrary decision. To whom love settles on the gravity that snares the sun. I ensnare the stars, and the moon begs for a dance. To whom a secret of many moons is disclosed."

"What is your name?"

"I am your past, your present, and your future. I need no name."

Ómalichanwa frowned. "Everyone and everything has a name."

"Many are the watchmen but not its antiquity. I am the beneath and above of living and dying in this realm and beyond."

Ómalichanwa sighed. Her instinct read nothing; this made her more concerned than alarmed. She didn't want this to drag into another night since she had seen her inevitable end. Decidedly, she roused and made her way to the entrance of the hut. As soon as she came out of the hut, she saw a fog, the colour of the moon. She cautiously walked into it. It was brighter inside with no edges like being surrounded by bright nothingness. The Ófòr-Oguneli was on the ground in pieces. She knew what to do, but not how to start.

"Follow your heart," the singing voice urged.

She nodded her thanks, unsure whether it was appropriate to say anything. She stretched her hand out to pick up the most significant piece of the Ófòr-Oguneli, and the memories of every past bearer flooded through her. While the memories of each bearer washed over her, her hands stitched the pieces together. She spent a few more hours recalling the nimbus veils of mist. Completing the rites for each nimbus veil, she sent them to their rightful heirs. Most of which she needed to create portals for.

Six nimbuses were missing, four of which were shielded, something seemed to be preventing their return. It cost her hours and a splitting headache, but she was done, and unlike her predecessors, she didn't have long to live. She'd had the privilege of seeing her death but not how it would unfold. Exhausted and sleepy, she still managed to complete the rites of transition. Finally finished, she stumbled out of the bubble of fog and into the hut with the Ófòr-Oguneli.

Just as she was about to lay her head down, she heard the music again and frowned. She had just answered Ófòr-Oguneli's call a few minutes ago. She tapped into the nimbus of hindsight and foresight and saw her death; it was to be by Okpararebisi in a few hours with the help of

97

Nwaneri. The revelation decreed their success. She prayed to the Lord of All for help. For if Nwaneri got the Ófòr-Oguneli, it would be the ending of the Twelve Kingdoms of Evóvuotu and the possible slavery of all living folks.

For some reason, as soon as her head touched the bamboo bed, she fell asleep but still felt awake. The further away she was from the Ófòr-Oguneli, the weaker she felt. Suspicious she decided to hold onto it.

"Greetings," the owl slurred. It was Nwaneri. The god-messenger had come to Evóvuotu in the form of an owl.

Ómalichanwa stepped out of the hut. Still drowsy, she leaned on the door frame. "What do you want?" she asked with no hint of malice.

"Give me that sceptre," Nwaneri ordered.

Ómalichanwa gave him a mirthless laugh.

"You shouldn't slight a god, you insolent youngling," he said pointedly, offended that a mortal would act with such irreverence.

Ómalichanwa nodded. She had to tread carefully; Nwaneri's twin was the god of mirth and festivity and associated with birth, peaceful death, weddings, and festivals. More so, she needed to stall him as she still hadn't located the nimbus of Harvest & Bloom, War & Servitude as well as four others. She hadn't done the three rites of transition for them.

Nwaneri blinked uncomfortably. He couldn't read her mind nor nudge her because Ófòr-Oguneli was protecting her, and he couldn't understand why. It was just a stick infused with powers. He would need his sibling's help for this and besides, it was his sibling's fault that he was in this predicament. Sometime soon, Awele would be awake, and that would spell doom for his promotion and diminish his chances of taking Omanma as his bride.

She turned sideways to look at him, only to see black,

98

round eyes staring at her. It was hard to know if he was angry with her. There was no expression on his face. Besides, she had never tried to read an animal's face before.

Nwaneri cocked his head left and right and blinked twice as he communicated with his sibling in the skies.

"There are more where that came from. Enjoy." He said. In a blink of an eye, an assortment of food was displayed on the floor. "I'll be back in the morning for the sceptre."

She squinted as a bright, silvery smoke cloud enveloped him and vanished with him. Relieved, she turned her concerned eyes to the Ófòr-Oguneli. In a few minutes, Okpararebisi would realise he was no longer in possession of the real Ófòr-Oguneli. She stalked back to the bed. She wanted to sleep, but the tapping sound kept interrupting her sleep. She roused herself, suddenly missing Isekó.

She closed her eyes in concentration. It was a heartbeat. She tapped into another nimbus to find the heartbeat and found it was the babeling in her aunt's womb, her aunt's labour had begun.

14.

Okpararebisi lividly stared at the pieces of Ófòr-Oguneli. After a while, he summoned the Chief Priest, who was conveniently out of town. Whingeing and moaning, he ordered his warriors to fetch him another chief priest. Enraged, he chased everyone out of his court including his new favourite, Ogbuogu. Not long after, the pieces of the Ófòr-Oguneli wavered. He went to examine it when a weefolk entered his court, but as he was about to blitz the weefolk, she removed the hide covering her head. He froze. Recollecting himself, he massaged his eyes and peered at the figure, vehemently willing it to be no illusion.

"Chinasa?" Okpararebisi gingerly whispered.

"It's I, Your Majesty!" she said with a small voice as she curtsied.

"O come, you don't need to bow to me," he rattled off.

"Why not? You're King," she retorted with a little chuckle.

He sighed; he'd missed that chuckle, a chuckle that always weakened his sour mood. Her hair was still black except for the specks of grey, and she walked tall. Intrigued at her youthfulness, he waited to ask her the many questions that reeled in his head. Seeing how painstakingly slow she moved, his desire to stall his age and hers improved greatly.

"Where have you been?" he eagerly asked.

"There," she gestured.

"Wha-at?"

"I've been at your gate," she murmured.

Okpararebisi incredulously shook his head. "It can't be! I search for you! I waited. I never stopped searching, and you tell me you were at the gate? Of this palace? My palace?"

"I've been a beggar, sitting at your gate for close to twenty cycles. I always returned after you chased us.

Okpararebisi sat beside her, looking remorseful.

"Who dishonours weefolks while waiting for his bride, Uzò?"

"It's not what you think!" Okpararebisi started. Alarmed at how much she knew and startled at her calling him by name - he'd almost forgotten he had one.

"You're the King why should what I think matter."

"Chinasa, don't talk like that, hear me out."

"Can you tuck a fallen feather back onto the bird?"

"Chinasa, please?"

"Why? Why would you violate weefolks, especially younglings with no dowry?" she asked, her voice shook as she trembled.

"May I explain?"

"Why childlings?"

"Never childling," he exclaimed, raising his hand to swear.

"I lived at your gate," she added pointedly.

Okpararebisi fell silent. He'd waited. He'd searched. She was here and was about to slip from his hand "I think something's wrong with me because I can't help it."

Sympathetic, Chinasa turned to face him. "Oche-Eze had no solution?"

"He said it will end when I choose a bride," he lied smoothly, averting his gaze.

"Oh, Uzò! Why then did you not take a bride?"

"Because of you. I wanted you and no other."

"But you knew that I had a mermate –"

"One that stole you from me," he spat and asked, "Where is he?"

"In the great beyond."

Okpararebisi frowned at her.

"He has joined our ancestors."

Okpararebisi waved his hands carelessly. "Well, I'm not sorry he's gone."

Chinasa wore a small smile as she shook her head.

"Childlings?" he asked curiously.

She shook her head again.

It must have been lonely without childlings, he thought and sighed. "I'm sorry."

"Don't be."

"Be my weemate."

Okpararebisi had said it so casually that she didn't think it was a question. It took a while for it to sink in. She slowly sat on one of the seats meant for titled men as she shook her head.

"Why not?"

"I'm good enough to be friends with, I'm too old and frail

to be a weemate."

"I've gotten a second chance, and I'll not lose."

She paused thoughtfully then asked; "Will it stop you from dishonouring the weefolks?"

"I swear it," he raised his hand and swore.

She pondered for a bit, nodded then rose from the seat kept strictly for elders.

"Where are you going?" he asked as he made to follow her.

Amused, she mumbled, "to ease myself."

Embarrassed, he lowered his head and stepped aside.

Soon after, she stepped out of his court, he summoned a guard so he could send him to fetch the elders. He turned to sit on the throne and saw the Ófòr-Oguneli waver again. He knew then that it was an illusion. As soon as the guard came in, he asked him to summon the warriors instead.

Chinasa returned to find several warriors in the court. She would have readily waited outside for their meeting to end. But couldn't help approaching the throne when she heard Okpararebisi words. Shocked and sullen at the level of hate in the words he spewed, she pushed through the crowd to get to him.

Okpararebisi saw Chinasa and fell silent.

She let tears stream down her face as released the nimbus that kept her youthful. And with a sigh, she breathed her last.

Ene'e appeared almost immediately. Okpararebisi looked on, curious and unperturbed as Ene'e took her away. He was now more concerned with getting the Ófòr-Oguneli; there was no saving Chinasa from the great beyond, she was now a lost cause. He could always mourn her later.

The morning draught wafted in while Ómalichanwa gathered what she needed to help her aunt with the birth.

Covering her de'nnâ, she added more sticks to the fire and slipped out of the hut. She got to her aunt's hut and found Ónu fast asleep beside his moaning weemate; cloaked herself in invisibility and whispered into his ear. Ónu dressed up quickly and left for the chief priest's compound, oblivious to his weemate. As soon as Ónu left, Ómalichanwa prepared her aunt for birthing while resisting the urge to let her aunt know her mermate's fate.

A few hours later, her nwónnénné gave birth to a boy childling. Ónu had chosen a name before the babeling was born, so he was named Akwu. As she carried the babeling to wrap him up, her mind sailed suddenly to Ónu. She wanted to avoid seeing it, but the nimbus insisted.

Ónu arrived at Oche-Eze's compound. He didn't hear the carnage because he was whistling. By the time he realised, it was too late, and an arrow was protruding from his belly. The King's guard searched Ónu's bag. They didn't know what they were supposed to be searching for, so they tugged his bag off him and ran back to the palace with what they had looted from the Chief Priest's hut.

Ómalichanwa touched her aunt's hand gently. "It is time. You must leave immediately."

Her aunt sighed grimly. She knew duty and also, hope. But she didn't want to leave Ónu and Ofia, her offspring, behind.

Ómalichanwa whirled her free hand, and all they'd need for a long journey tucked themselves into sacks, in all the huts at the same time excluding Ónu's first weemate's huts. Averting her eyes while her aunt got dressed, Ómalichanwa's tears trickled down on the babeling's cheek, and she quickly wiped them off. Liking an idea that popped in her head, she shared her powers to the babeling, knowing that the transfer would be complete upon her death. Right after she understood why she couldn't shake off the pull of the nimbus of Comfort & Solace. The youngest member of the family was its Paramount Ruler. His nwónnenanna, Jeóma was already a Paramount Ruler of Healing and Protection and wise beyond her years. She handed her cousin to his nné and guided them outside, and then she touched her aunt to heal her.

Her aunt gave her a questioning look, shrugged, and went to the adjoining hut to wake her offspring. While she was exiting the adjoining hut, Ónu's first weemate came out of her hut but returned when a babeling cried out.

"Nwô'm, my senior is awake early today," Ómalichanwa's aunt whispered to her because her childlings and maids were with her.

"I noticed," Ómalichanwa mumbled with a nod. "The babeling will keep her busy for some time. Do you trust your maids?"

She shrugged.

"Ask them," Ómalichanwa urged.

She called her maids in one at a time to ask them and watched Ómalichanwa's reaction to each of them. Out of the five, Ómalichanwa approved of one, but that one insisted on going to see her ailing mother. Thinking of the babeling, she took back the first two and sent the rest away. They cried because their mistress had refused to tell them what they'd done wrong and wailed when she insisted that they'd done nothing wrong. Meanwhile, Ómalichanwa called her de'nnâ with her mind. He came to her aunt's hut and nodded his greetings to his late weemate's nwónnenanna.

Afterwards, Ómalichanwa went to the path that they had taken to get to Ónu's compound. While she was out in the semi-forest scouting for the leaves she'd need for the ritual, she sent thoughts of prayers to noble hearts. She was hard at work soon after she returned.

Eriri got up to ease himself and found his offspring

furiously crushing odd leaves and seeds on a grinding stone. He suspiciously glanced at the three large itès hanging over firewood, wondering why she set them so far apart, at different positions and what was cooking in them. Knowing how much she hated being interrupted, he waited. A few minutes later, a leopard, two hares, a rabbit, a squirrel, four hyenas, and three foxes as white as clouds on a sunny day came forth. Eriri quickly went for his flinchete, but when he returned to find her greeting them, he stayed his hand. He rubbed his forehead and shook his head. He had seen too many weird things too soon and wondered how his offspring was faring. But like her nné, it would be easier to pry tears from a stone. He had a lot of questions but was willing to wait for when she'd be willing to entertain them.

The leaves Ómalichanwa hadn't crushed she took with her into the hut she'd slept in. She'd chosen the hut because it was at the edge of Onu's compound and it faced the north wind.

Eriri was so distracted that he'd forgotten why he came out in the first place until his bladder warned. He hurried to the latrine and returned to find Ómalichanwa and Jeóma having a conversation. He couldn't hear what was said; his discomfort heightened because he liked to be in the know. Helplessness weighed his brows down. Shaking his head, he left the hut.

Soon after Jeóma left, Ómalichanwa went in and out of the hut several times, casting a spell each time. The animals that arrived earlier entered the hut except for the foxes, and with eyes fixed on her, they crouched at a corner of the hut. She prepared to open a portal that would take her family out of El'ikenueze, but unsure of a destination, she called to memories of some past bearers of a few nimbuses in Ófòr-Oguneli and took the one that looked farthest away from the palace Kingdom.

Realising she had forgotten something, she hurried to her aunt's hut. There, she made the Ófòr-Oguneli small enough to fit into her palm in a bid to disguise it then tucked it in a satchel after wrapping it. She heard footsteps approach and gasped. Even though her spirit-guide had told her who it was, she still couldn't help fidgeting. As soon as Jeóma entered the hut, Ómalichanwa gave the satchel to her and hurried out of the hut with Jeóma following closely.

Ómalichanwa's heart raced from fear and trepidation. It was only when she began to shudder in terror that her spirit-guide came to console her. Calmer, she slanted her head to greet her aunt then sat in the space her de'nnâ had kept for her.

They all sat outside waiting for the maids to finish cleaning the hut - it was customary to do so after the birth of a babeling.

"Mama, what's his name?" Jeóma asked her nné as she brought her sibling to her.

Tears gathered in Jeóma's nné's eyes. She was worried about Ofia, his inventions had taken him to Rumuochara, and she had no way of sending him a message.

"We must leave," Ómalichanwa whispered hoarsely.

Her nwónnenanna sighed. She wanted to stay, but her instincts had never failed her. Looking at the new babeling, she sighed again, more determined. "His name will be Akwu,"

"Akwu," Jeóma said, wearing a confused smile. "It's quite an unusual thing to name a babeling after a nut."

"We must leave!" Ómalichanwa said more urgently and walked back to the hut she'd shared with her de'nnâ.

Eriri returned to the hut and was almost knocked down by the wind. Alarmed, he called to his offspring as it was too windy to open his eyes. He shoved his flinchete into the ground to keep him grounded against the force of the wind. When he opened his eyes, he saw his offspring's mouth moving with her eyes closed and knew she was the source of the wind.

She had created a portal which looked like an opening in the wall, an opening much like she'd done before, On the other side of the portal was greenery like he'd never seen before. It was lush with specks of colours. The portal she'd created was much bigger than the last and it seemed to have sapped her energy because she fell back. Luckily, caught her albeit by the head. Letting her rest, he quickly called his late weemate's nwónnenanna.

Ómalichanwa practically shoved everyone into the portal. When everyone got in, she pretended to be doing an incantation.

"Mpa, go on. I need to finish this."

Eriri frowned, a little hesitant to leave her behind then nodded. "Okay, but hurry."

As soon as her de'nnâ went through, she moved to seal the portal, but the leaves weren't with her. She took a long look at her de'nnâ as she tried to fight back tears. Sighing, she blew a gentle breeze to fill his heart with comfort and asked Jeóma to seal the portal then crumbled to the floor, crying. One of the foxes came into the hut and rubbed its nose on her shoulder, she leaned on it and cried until she was exhausted.

She quickly hurried outside to the itès on the fire, set them aside then knocked down the stand that had held the itès above the fire. She used the pieces of the stand to draw

a line around the hut using her hand to gauge the depth of the line. As soon as it was deep enough to cover her wrist, she poured the content of each itès into the lines she'd created, starting with the one furthest from the hut.

There was a spark on the ground along the line followed by a ripple in the air. She had barely finished the last – which was in the hut - when the foxes began to growl. They flanked her as she stepped out of the hut. Okpararebisi was standing there, Ónu's first weemate stood adjacent to him, her arms akimbo, a satisfied smile on her face. Some other people also gathered around them. Everyone else was on their knees except for the warriors.

Eriri suspecting something was wrong ran into the portal with one hand on his sheath but fell through to the other side of the marshland they were standing on.

She has sealed it, he thought and fell on his knees.

Eriri hadn't allowed himself to do so since her nné had died, but now he let loose, forgetting that there was no pride in a merfolk crying. His helplessness made him feel like a coward, not defending his offspring when he was supposed to. Almost immediately, he felt warm like he was covered in bear-fur and abruptly got up, wondering why he was crying like a weefolk and why he was on his knees. Sheathing his flinchete, he walked ahead of the group tugging the cart bearing their belongings as he tried to find their location. He was unable to shake off the feeling that he'd forgotten something.

15.

Okpararebisi tried to break the walls of her mind in his attempt to control her. Something threw him off. It felt like an invisible wall kept him out so he couldn't cross the threshold of the hut. A wall much like the one he'd created around the palace kingdom but he hadn't sensed any pearl from the Oko River or he would have dislodged it. He suspected it was the herbs that gleamed off her skin. Frustrated, he ordered that the hut be burned down, but the wall stood in the warriors' path. Okpararebisi snorted, knowing it was something he could take care of by getting rid of her.

Unsuccessful with banishing the formidable wall, he sat on a badly hewn slab of wood near the udala tree opposite the hut and let out a mirthless laugh. He could sense Ófòr-Oguneli, but it felt distant. He was impressed with the Lord of All's choice of a bane: a girl childling. He was as intrigued as he was annoyed that though the Ófòr-Oguneli recognised him, it chose to protect her. It had never protected him; he didn't even know it could do that.

A cloud of smoke appeared behind him and withdrew to reveal Nwaneri in the form of an owl. After a silent debate, Okpararebisi got up and dismantled the first wall. The second wall was quite tricky, it wavered like an illusion, but he couldn't find a weakness in it. Irritated, he spun to glare at the owl, which clung to the guava tree. It blinked a few times and Okpararebisi grimaced. Reluctantly, he muttered his thanks and quickly decimated the second wall.

He rushed to the third barrier so impatiently and forcefully that his glamour wavered, startling the warriors, palace guards, and some of the weefolks who had come with him. For a complete second, they saw an old merfolk, knobbly and bent-over, some of his teeth had yellowed, and some were completely gone, his white hair stuck out from various parts of his shiny head.

Ómalichanwa closed her eyes and spoke to the beasts that guarded her with her mind. When she opened her eyes, something glimmered, and she blinked. Taking a closer look, she discovered that Okpararebisi was wearing a glamour that made him look much younger than his true self; although he wasn't holding a cane he was bent over, and his back and chest were covered in white hair.

Her spirit-guide's ideas filtered into her thoughts, and she returned her attention to the task at hand. In sharing her powers with Akwu, she had inadvertently doubled his life span and the lives of other Okoruchi. It was the only thing she could think of to prevent Okpararebisi from continuing his life of tyranny. She hoped she could wait him out until high noon. He was desperate, and Nwaneri had helped him get past the first barrier she created. In a matter of minutes, he would get past the second barrier, but the third had taken the most time to secure. She silently prayed that the second one would be tricky enough to delay his access to the third.

A sharp pain pierced her heart, dispersed wildly through her body and disappeared in an instant. Shrugging it off, she concentrated on improving the protective bubble she had created around herself, then it happened again. Okpararebisi may not have the Ófòr-Oguneli, but he still had residual powers from being in contact with it for so long.

Worry about dying distracted her even more with the pain. She heard a hissing sound behind her and jumped. She wanted to run away and spun to find that the portal was no longer open. Trying to focus on good thoughts, she looked down, wrinkling her nose as she farted. She still couldn't help glances back and forth, between the entrance of the hut where her nemesis approach was looming and the back of the hut where the portal once was. Not only did she stink, but she also looked grotesquely green. She'd lathered her body with various herbs including the juice of a young plantain stalk to ward off Okpararebisi's powers.

Okpararebisi undid the glamour. He licked his lips hungrily as he stared at her soft, parted lips and long slender neck. She reminded him of the youngling that shattered the Ófòr-Oguneli. Her languid eyes were now closed as she concentrated on keeping him out of her head. He nodded his approval; she wasn't much of a youngling but was quite pretty. He made a mental note to ravish her as soon as he got what he wanted, for now, he just had to distract her, as

Nwaneri had advised. He played with his bushy moustache, looked back at Nwaneri, then at her.

"You think you can stop me?" He coaxed.

"I'm in no position to stop you, Your Majesty!" Ómalichanwa retorted as calmly as she could, tucking her shaky hands behind her as she curtsied.

"Mhm," He nodded with brows raised and crossed his arms. "Why all the walls then?"

"A maiden must protect herself, Your Majesty," she mumbled and thinned her lips.

He smiled slightly. "You are a beautiful youngling," he said smoothly with a very gentle voice.

She gulped, and just then, a sharp pain pierced her head. She thought of her de'nnâ, but each memory she came up with faltered. None was strong enough to keep him out of her head. The pain increased so much so she could think of nothing else but the pain.

The other animals nuzzled the foxes and breathed their last as their life-forces were transferred into the foxes. The foxes grew larger almost immediately. They growled as they advanced to defend her, their fur stood tall and moved like glistening ripples. They were indeed the silent foxes of Agbalanya Forest. For as their fur glistened, it rippled, like the leaves on the path of the wind. They were powerful enough to weaken Okpararebisi's torture.

Okpararebisi whirled his hands, and a fireball appeared on each palm. Laughing like a mad merfolk, he trashed at the third barrier. The energy ball that came out of his hand sparked, sizzled and turned to ash each time it came in contact with the barrier. The ground shook from the impact, but the barrier did not budge. However, it left smudges that looked like dirt frozen in the air. He gritted his teeth and turned to Nwaneri, but Nwaneri was no longer hanging from the guava tree.

Amid the pain, Ómalichanwa sensed something else. An unsettling cold began to overwhelm her, starting at her feet. The foxes and the hyena started acting restless, but their restlessness was covered by fear. Only one being could administer that much fear: the King of Rimeóku, but there was something off about the odourless scent. Whatever being it was, it left as quickly as it came. She frowned, wondering.

There was a loud bang from a distance that echoed around everyone within the palace Kingdom and ceased.

Okpararebisi stopped suddenly and tilted his head. He frowned unsure of hearing the drum, but he noticed the change in the atmosphere. *There's something strange in the air, something unfamiliar. Wrong.* Defiant, he stretched, determined to get hold of Ófòr-Oguneli.

It became eerily quiet. The foxes no longer growled but remained alert, their head low in curtsey. The birds outside had stopped chirping making her wonder how long they'd been fighting. Her wonder was brief. She could sense something coming. Something unfamiliar. Something that her instinct warned against. She looked up with a nimbus. The sky was clear, but the sun had disappeared.

Okpararebisi looked up. Crows and ravens appeared from thin air and circled. As they circled their numbers increased, and so did the speed of their descent. They circled until they formed a mass of black cloud high above the hut. Lightning struck and flashed in the middle of the black cloud then the birds dipped like a whirlwind pointed at him. He raised his hand to shield himself, an invisible barrier came over him like a shield. A forceful wind swept through the compound. He wobbled and fell on the wall he'd been trying to dismantle. It sparked, merging with his shield. He laughed maniacally and waved a hand at Ómalichanwa.

Ómalichanwa's vision became blurry as the pain in her

head doubled. The only thing that separated her from Okpararebisi was the protective bubble around her, but it had weakened. The shadow cast by the birds made it almost impossible to see. She could just about make out Okpararebisi's silhouette as he continued to shield himself from the diving birds. As she began to black out, she felt a prickly itch and inched away from Okpararebisi then felt warmth around her chest. It was followed by the sense of being pulled into a small space, and her mind went blank. She blinked as she tried to adjust her eyes to the sudden brightness. Finally, opening her eyes, her de'nnâ was beside her, smiling. Wondering why she couldn't recall any such memory, she blinked again and squinted.

Jeóma pinched her.

Looking at Jeóma, she realised it wasn't a memory.

"Your de'nnâ insisted," Jeóma offered casually as she produced limp leaves from her pocket.

Eriri feigned anger. "The charm you used on me didn't last."

"It wasn't a charm," she replied with a small smile then tried to sit up, but her aunt pushed her back.

"I have to go back, or all will be lost!" She spoke to no one in particular, but her eyes held a plea.

"You don't need to," Jeóma said with her glowing hands wrapped around Ómalichanwa's head.

Ómalichanwa gave in to the drowsy warmth of Jeóma's healing hands for a few seconds, then shook herself out of it. "No," she cried and swatted Jeóma's hands. "Stop it!"

While they hovered and fussed over Ómalichanwa, one of the maids went to the portal that Jeóma had reopened and was now pulling Okpararebisi towards it. The other maid set the baby down and went to assist her friend before the portal closed.

"Where has that youngling gone again?" Ómalichanwa's

nwónnenanna muttered under her breath when the babeling started crying. She got up and walked over to the babeling. "Look!" she squealed, pointing at the portal.

Jeóma instantly whirled her hand casting a spell of protection.

Okpararebisi saw her and flicked his fingers; dust from the ground swirled into arrows and came through the portal, breaking the shield she had just about formed.

Startled, Jeóma moved back and stumbled over Ómalichanwa.

Ómalichanwa sat up. She looked at her de'nnâ and down to where the cocoyam leaves were and nodded. Her de'nnâ tilted his head slightly, ready to peel the cocoyam leaves like she had done the first time they used a portal together. Ómalichanwa looked back at the portal; she had to think quickly. If she closed the portal, he would use the maid to find a way back to them. Just then she wished Jeóma had not opened it.

The shield! Her spirit-guide whisper in her thought. *Harbingers of Death! The gods had passed judgement! Let them through! Now!*

She couldn't stay, she cried through her thoughts and the little distraction wobbled the bubble. Then she heard the cawing of the birds as they continued to peck at the barriers she'd created. *What about the shield?* She asked her spirit guide.

What about the shield? Ómalichanwa asked again. Receiving no answer, she restlessly pondered. The portal was her access to the shield she had built so she stopped Jeóma from tearing the leaves. She started to sing and weave a counter-spell to undo the barriers, as quickly and as steadily as possible then paused.

Okpararebisi was close to the portal, ready to make his

escape.

Wearing a worried frown, she continued to undo the spell then the wind blew sand into her eyes and an idea struck her. Thanking the Lord of All for her luck, she closed her eyes and summoned the shield to her.

16.

Jeóma finally completed another protection spell. It wrapped everyone in an invisible bubble, except herself and Ómalichanwa; she feared it would disrupt Ómalichanwa's activity.

As soon as Ómalichanwa was able to focus on the shield, she started to pull it to her through the portal.

Okpararebisi got wind of her intention as she had forgotten to put a barrier to her thoughts. He smirked flicking a hand, and she found her mind retreating within her. Not long after, a feeling of being pulled underwater overwhelmed her when Okpararebisi clenched his hand into a fist.

There was an invisible restraint, one she couldn't break. The second she became afraid, something came and nudged her. The fear increased exponentially, causing her to cower and recede into the inner chambers of her mind. Fear had taken over her faculties so that she couldn't think. She had never experienced anything like it. It didn't taunt her, just wrapped itself around her like a clam around its pearl. The more she fought, the more afraid she became until she was crippled with fear.

Okpararebisi smiled and blew air into his fist. All the while ignoring the crows and ravens.

It was the first time Jeóma had used her powers, so she didn't know what to do. She peered at Ómalichanwa as Ómalichanwa grew weaker. Her grandmother had once told her that when something was queer she should start with what she knew. Without another thought, she linked her hands with Ómalichanwa's. She was too nervous to concentrate. Jeóma felt a push and closed her eyes to help her focus.

Ómalichanwa shuddered from the vibration within her. It started from her heart and grew. As the glow increased, the jagged edges of the mist that engulfed her began to hiss and retreat. After a while, she began to feel like she was floating, then heard Jeóma beckoning her, and as she gulped for air, she came through, sneezing. Somewhere between anger and irritation, she grounded her mind and focused on the shield. She felt Jeóma in her head, prancing and ready to pounce as she built a mind shield like she had never seen before.

Jeóma was so focused on building the mind shield for Ómalichanwa that she forgot to complete the enchantment to maintain the protection spell. Okpararebisi, seeing the shield waver, tossed a spear at her. It hit her just above her breast; she fell back, undoing her link with Ómalichanwa.

Ómalichanwa got up abruptly, her head reeled. Twisting her mouth to the side and wrinkling her nose, she squinted and put all her might into pulling the shield in her direction. Okpararebisi was close to the portal, her aunt's maids beside him. From the corner of her eyes, she could see her de'nnâ struggling to break the bubble, the large cocoyam leaf that was to be used to seal the portal still in his hand.

Ómalichanwa slanted her head and saw a glimpse of an opportunity when Okpararebisi lowered his hands. She tilted her head, and Okpararebisi flew across the hut with the maids landing atop of him. She inhaled deeply and blew whirlwind into the portal and began to make whorls with her hand so that as soon as Okpararebisi swatted it, a thick fog replaced it. She quickly ran to her de'nnâ and placed her palm on the shield and nodded. Eriri touched the cocoyam leaf to the palm of her hand from inside the bubble, the leaf permeated the bubble and onto her palm. The bubble remained unscathed.

As she ran back her hand glowed, wilting the leaf. Quickly, she tore it to pieces, tucked it into her chest piece. The fog started clearing just as she pulled the shield down. The force of the shield passing through the portal caused her to flop like a leaf in the wind. She dug a foot in the ground and spun to toss the shield farther away from her. The round shield was of an overwhelming size much like the bubble but with sturdy walls; the force of the energy used sent it flying a long way away.

The birds perched at Okpararebisi weakening him, so he used one of the maids as a shield and used the other to create a path to the portal.

Ómalichanwa quickly tossed the pieces of leaves on the ground, sealing the portal. Okpararebisi hit a wall, but one of his legs made it through before it closed. Confused, she looked on; she had no right to harm him, especially since the god-touch was on him. She nodded her head, settled in the belief that they had somehow come to the rescue. It was their choice to send the crows and the ravens so he wouldn't have an afterlife. Transfixed, her eagerness to see the end of the destruction overshadowed her repulsion. Each bird pecking at him was the size of a well-fed chicken. They tugged his leg out of the spot in the portal that remained open. One of the crows was all black, unlike the other ones with white chests and necks, pecked at the opening of the portal, filling it up. She couldn't make him out through the birds fluttering around. Then the portal disappeared.

Exhausted, relieved and excited, Ómalichanwa crumbled to the ground then jumped when she felt something touch her bottom. Slanting her head, she saw

118

Jeóma's chest wound and leaned over her but couldn't find a heartbeat. Tears streamed down the side of her face. Her fate was inevitable. Jeóma had only delayed it. She quietly whispered and the bubbles shielding her de'nnâ, Jeóma's nné and nnéruka fizzled away.

Eriri touched the spear, and it turned to the dust it was made of. Her nwónnenanna set Akwu aside to put pressure on the wound. Ómalichanwa pressed Jeóma's hand to the injury and urged Jeóma to heal herself. She took her de'nnâ's hand and pressed it on Jeóma's hand to hold it in place while she rummaged through Jeóma's bag in search of any herb. Tears streamed down her face again, but she brushed them off. She had seen this future, and she knew what to do. She exhaled deeply and moved to stand next to her de'nnâ, while Jeóma's nné was crumbled over her offspring's body.

"Papa," she called and turned her de'nnâ's face to hers, then whispered, "it is time."

"For?" Eriri mumbled, then his face registered shock as what she hadn't put into words dawned on him. "Why am I not shaken?"

"Because you're better prepared now."

"You're all I have."

"No, you have her." Ómalichanwa tilted her head to her aunt.

"Them. You mean them." He glanced at his late weemate's nwónnenanna, then the babeling, and crumbled.

Ómalichanwa trudged slowly towards Jeóma. She held both Jeóma's hands over her chest and chanted. Where their hands merged, their hands began to glow until it was as bright as the sun then she pressed their hands to Jeóma's chest. Jeóma heaved; her body jerked a few times as her life-force was restored.

A few minutes later, Ene'e appeared and caught

Ómalichanwa as she slumped.

In Rumuigodo, a mountain rose from where the Awele's granule hit the ground and the crate was covered in yellow dust. The grounds shook as the grain cooked. Thick black smoke billowed, the mountain split to reveal seven jagged edges. For days, in the realm of the gods, Awele shuddered in his stupor. The tremors could be felt at all ends of the Twelve Kingdoms then the ground at most of the boundaries, and across some villages split open. The jagged gaps were too wide to cross. a lot of farmers were returning at the time the earthquake started.

Awele's planned to bury the palace Kingdom so no heir would rise from that compound, but the granule landed a far way off in another kingdom.

As the ground trembled, Ene'e sniffed the air and shook his head.

"What was that?" Eriri asked as he looked around in search of the King's guards.

"Awele has spoken," Ene'e explained.

Soon after, the ground split open, separating Ene'e, Jeóma, Ómalichanwa and Akwu from their parents, Jeóma woke up. She saw her nné at the edge of the tear in the ground which was a few paces wide. Fearing that he'll fall into the gap, Jeóma stretched her hand to catch him, and his skin burned from her touch, scarring him. The ground shook again, and the gap widened. She quickly opened her hands like she was cradling something fragile.

A bubble enveloped him.

She guided it over the gap until it landed on her nné's outstretched arms, then she cupped her palm and whispered, opening her hand. She did it twice and waved her hand. Two invisible bubbles sailed across to her uncle and her nné simultaneously, then she collapsed.

Ene'e turned to see the grieving parents. He bowed slightly, still carrying Ómalichanwa's lifeless body, he moved closer to Jeóma, shimmered and disappeared with them. Soon after he left a plant erupted from the ground. It was believed that such a plant grew in the spot where a great sacrifice was made. To this day, the plant exists and only the one with the god-touch could make it blossom so long as he or she is related to the sacrifice.

Revenge by Default

Onuma hated reunions.

Everyone smiled sweetly, but their eyes judged. It was an unrivalled competition; from who wore the most expensive outfit to whose husband was the most powerful. She was always the worst dressed of course. Who could blame her? She was saving two-thirds of her salary for her perfect wedding whenever it will happen.

Her mother had warned her not to make her a topic of discussion at the next Christian Mothers' Meeting. She even advised Onuma to hire a man to stand by her side at the wedding if possible. Onuma did try, but most of the men she knew were from work, and they were either married or separated. The single ones seem to dread wedding ceremonies.

She knew what was coming if she attended Abigail's wedding, but she had to. It was, after all, her sister's wedding. She was going to be twenty-nine in two weeks, Abigail, who was good at usurping her, fixed her wedding for that day. Who else would set their wedding on their spinster sister's birthday? But Abigail, her showy sister, wanted to remind everyone that as a twenty-year-old undergraduate she had acquired for herself a husband who happened to be a bank manager in his twenties.

She shouldn't feel bad. After all, she had rejected the man her father chose for her after he had done the traditional introduction rites and decided to go to the university. She should be glad to be a trendsetter since after her rebellion other girls in the community chose to go to university before settling down.

Onuma wasn't sad. She was bitter.

She wasn't the prettiest girl in town, but she wasn't the

most mundane either. At twenty-nine she had a doctorate and a good job and was desperate enough to date her boss. She almost went to the registry to marry him until a woman showed up claiming to be his wife. That was six months ago.

Her only consolation had come from *Sumptuous Cakes Galleria*. The new habit gave her a voluptuous backside, a well-rounded stomach, and chubby arms. She was going to her sister's wedding without a man. To cap it off, she was going to be her sister's bridesmaid. Her entire family knew her male friends - her father had made it his duty.

She stared at her reflection and kissed her teeth. Who *would be willing to stand by my side? I'm a blunt, opinionated woman: a rebel by chivalric standard.* Sighing, she grimaced then smiled ruefully as she played with her plummeting stomach, lifting it and letting it sag. Still baffled at how rapidly she gained the weight, decided to toss out any ice cream, éclairs or chocolate in the freezer. With two weeks to get in shape for the wedding, two stones in two months didn't seem possible. She turned to her side to gauge the size of her stomach, sucking it in.

Abigail was obsessed with the numbers three and nine. She needed nine bridesmaids. She was one short because one of her bridesmaids was suddenly unavailable. Anything Abigail wanted, Abigail got. Her mother had blackmailed her into wearing the bridesmaid dress Abigail had picked.

Onuma hated being laid out on display, like a chunk of meat at a butcher's shop. But her father believed it would help her get noticed and hoped it would boost her chances of getting married. She also hoped their plan worked, because she was desperate for a man of her own. She was tired of being alone.

Ejiro, her best friend and colleague, had called to let her know she had a solution to the *bulging* situation. The flowing dress could cover a lot of discrepancies except the

123

bridesmaid dress was two sizes too small. She looked like a pregnant woman in the dress – that would definitely spark a new kind of scandal. The neckline was a little too low for her barely-there breasts. It was going to need padding.

Ejiro arrived thirty minutes later with three black outfits that looked like swimsuits. One stretched to the knee. The lower part of the other two was shaped like panties. Two of them had straps. With Ejiro's help, she was able to get into two of them before pulling the dress on. She arched her back; it was hard to stand otherwise.

The wedding day finally came. Grey clouds shawled the sky was covered in grey clouds. Onuma carried an umbrella in case it rained. She had forgotten that she might need to sit down until she got into her car. When she got to the church, she was stiff from sitting upright and her legs wobbled from numbness. One of the pads underneath her breast was beginning to show. An usher descended on her with a purple shawl that clashed with the cobalt blue dresses of the wedding party. It smelled of stale breast milk and also smelled like a baby that hadn't been bathed in days.

Abigail slid her a look with her teeth clenched from under her veil, which said *'you better die right now'*. Onuma twisted her mouth, feigning ignorance. In a funny way, she always did seem to steal the show. She hadn't eaten since yesterday, and her stomach let out its third growl. It was quite loud but went unnoticed because everyone was up and milling about.

The wedding ceremony started promptly - typical of orthodox gatherings. Onuma heard groaning and creaking as people got up or shifted for the latecomers. Her thighs hurt from not being able to sit properly, and she was beginning to feel lightheaded that she was relieved when the ceremony finally ended.

The photoshoot went by without a hitch. The sky

darkened immediately after and everyone scrambled to the reception venue at the back of her uncle's house. The rain fell after the opening prayer. While the guests were safely tucked away from the rain, Onuma was forced to leave the canopy to get her aunt's cane and her grandmother's snuff box. It was already raining heavily, that by the time she got to the house, some spokes in her umbrella were bent and she was utterly sodden. Her dress clung to her body. Fortunately, the bodyshapers were seamless. After giving her aunt and grandmother their items, she turned to make a quick exit and bumped into her father.

Onuma's father tucked her hand in his and began to parade her. She walked stiffly beside him as he introduced her to every man, young and old, as long as he was single. Half of them leered and ogled her. She didn't blame them. They should see her without that many bodyshapers - when she looked like an advertisement for Michelin tyres.

She raised a hand to her head; her vision was getting blurry. She couldn't risk eating or sitting down, so she staggered towards the exit and stumbled on a length of rope. Some of the teenagers that sat near the rear of the tent came to assist her. They tugged the rope so hard that it didn't only break the heel of her shoe but took down half of the tent that was behind their high table.

Onuma gasped and scuttled to a seat near the exit before anyone would notice her as the culprit. The master of ceremony was still cracking jokes, but people were no longer laughing. Their hanging jaws caused the bride to follow their gaze. Then the DJ lowered the volume on the music to find out what the problem was.

In the captivated silence, the sound of Onuma's uncle grunting and the maid cooing filled the tent; "yes, like that, oh yes, mh-huh."

Fortunately, children had their own tent.

Onuma slid down further into a chair far away from the scene and was typing into her phone, and though her head was low, she could see her sister bury her face in her hands. Everyone else seemed frozen in time, except for her grandmother, who picked up the part of the canopy on the ground and threw it over the couple in sexual congress. It was only then that they stopped. Her uncle couldn't look in their direction, instead he walked briskly towards the nearest exit, dragging the girl who was already crying.

Onuma looked over at her uncle's wife, but the woman seemed oblivious to what had just taken place. She was partially deaf, but her head lolled to one side. Probably drunk again or just sleeping.

Meanwhile, one of the teenagers who'd helped her was talking to her mother, who now batted her eyes at her older daughter, viciously. She twisted her mouth, hoping the teenager wasn't telling on her. She'd been sure that no one had seen her. Her mother would have gorged her eyes out had she been sitting beside her.

Onuma's uncle was barely out of sight when a boisterous woman came lunging towards the high table. The woman was pointing at Abigail's husband. "So it is true! You married another woman, *abi*? Useless man..."

"Who is this?" Abigail asked her husband in a loud whisper.

"Taah, who are you? You think you can snatch my husband?"

"Husband?" Abigail gasped and turned to face the groom. "Honey, what is she talking about?"

The groom slouched and cleared his throat noisily.

Abigail's hands were shaking as she hysterically tapped her husband. "You're not saying anything." He winced and loosened his tie but didn't get up.

Abigail nudged him violently. "Say something!"

"He has nothing to say because it is true." The woman spat and then turned to the groom. "Did I lie?"

Abigail shook him, pleading.

The boisterous woman, by this time, had moved behind the table and was walking towards them. As soon as the woman closed the gap between them, he got up half-running to the exit, and the boisterous woman chased after him. Onuma's mother undid her huge *gele* - head tie - and covered her face with it. Her father was fuming, his nostrils flared. Luckily, his gaze was fixed on Abigail. Apart from Onuma's grandmother, no one else cared about the man having coitus with the maid. The rotund woman whose hand was hooked in the belt of the groom as he tried to make a quick exit seemed to be a more interesting taboo.

 Onuma was overcome with the urge to urinate. She got one of the boys to get her a taxi. She looked around surreptitiously, snagged two bottles of wine from the table closest to her, before slipping out. As soon as she got close to the hotel, her bladder could no longer wait. She hurriedly pulled out a five hundred naira note from her purse and tossed it at the driver then ran across the lobby to her room.

She struggled to get out of the bodyshapers, but it was too late to hold back, so she sat in the bath and let go. It was only then that she realised that she'd forgotten to collect four hundred naira from the taxi driver. She sighed, removed the bodyshapers, and turned on the shower.

An hour later, she was in the bathtub with an open bottle of wine on the bedside table as she flipped through the channels for a romantic movie. She raised the bottle and took a sip then filled a champagne flute.

"Serves my sister right for fixing her wedding on my birthday. Maybe I'll go and console her tomorrow, but today

127

belongs to me."

She raised the champagne flute.

Happy birthday to me!

Hope on the Bumpy Road

The truth was that I was tired - tired of living from hand to mouth, looking at the time and urging the days to ebb away, searching the ground and hoping desperately that someone had dropped a fiver.

I can't go job hunting because my visa has expired.

I applied for a renewal of my visa a few months too late. I can't secure a job without a letter acknowledging this, so I'm not eligible to work, and only a *gonzo* can employ me under the pressure of a £10,000 fine. As if that wasn't enough, I hear there is a three-year backlog on applications. Three years.

Meanwhile, I've been squatting at my best friend Trish's place. Trish is a petite Nigerian with silvery blonde hair and facial features which always reminds me of Jet Li. I've been thinking of what will happen to me when she relocates to her home country in a few weeks. Meanwhile, Bola, who's able to help, needs her husband's permission since I'm not a relative. My only option now is to squat with an acquaintance whose offer of unsentimental copulation I've turned down numerous times.

With no family around, I've texted everybody I knew could pull up some financial strings, but they expect something in return. One was nice enough to give me some bloated hope by asking for my account number only to etch an enormous blight in my ticker, having never sent any money to my account. No one seems to know the meaning of "nothing ventured; nothing gained" anymore. I'm skint in every sense of the word.

I had £3.10 cash and 30p in my account. In other words, my "home and abroad" is £3.40. My eyes glazed with tears when I thought of what could have been.

Not long ago, I sat at the bus stop waiting for the bus that would carry me anywhere but here. I think I nodded off because someone woke me up just as the bus arrived. I got onto the bus and only then discovered that the bus fare had been increased by 50p, and even if I had my debit card with me, I couldn't possibly withdraw 30p from a cash machine. Flushed with embarrassment, I climbed down and turned away until the bus drove off.

Last Saturday, I decided I needed to take a breather. I got ready to go out of the house, a habit I disdained the past weeks. I wore a blue floral print tunic that I bought from *Dorothy Perkins* seven fashion seasons ago, because the dusty pink long-sleeve sweater was a bit too faded and the blue skinny jeans were frayed between the thighs. After combing my hair, I rifled through the wardrobe and picked up my best friend's cream-coloured waterfall cardigan with a scowl-like neckline. It was the only item of clothing she had that I could fit into since I was a more profound dress size than her, though my batwings were much slenderer than hers.

By the time I got to the Town Centre, the shops were open. I looked up at the mannequin used to display summer clothes and longed to get one. For the first time in my life, I did some window shopping and saw the price tag and suddenly I didn't even feel weird wearing clothes that were so out of date. I bumped into one of my former classmates on my way out of one of the shops. I felt smug after we hugged because she told me I smelled nice. She didn't know that I was wearing the last drop of the perfume I owned.

It was a sunny day, so I decided to take a long walk. The wind blew lightly across the old town. I heard the rustling leaves and extended my wall towards the Old Tanlaw Mill and sighed at the clueless serene beauty. I sat on the green, rusted bench situated close to the bank of a watercourse and stared dreamily at the water as it drifted unerringly and wished I was the one floating away. I felt calm and drowsy...

It was dark when I woke up. I took a surreptitious squint around as I walked on the tiny path leading to a bridge. Seeing no one, I bent down, gathered some leaves into my arms and threw them into the air. I did it several times, laughing then stopped suddenly because I noticed someone standing a few feet away.

"Please don't stop on my account," the person said, laughing and walking towards me. He wasn't familiar, but I wasn't scared of him, and neither was my guard up.

The brown leaves suddenly felt like dirt. I quickly dropped them and rubbed my palms to remove any

131

residue. I didn't know what to say nor want to say anything. I scratched the back of my head and started walking away, well towards him as that was the only way the shortest route to my hostel.

He cleared his throat and said, "I could use the company."

I sized him up, shrugged, and waited.

He walked towards me with a slanted look. He stopped a few inches away and shoved his hand in his pocket. "You're not going to say anything, are you?"

I shrugged and smiled.

"You're not in the mood..." He peered at me. "Well then, I'll do all the talking. My name is Earl." He pointed at me, laughing when I frowned at him. "I got you there, didn't I? You know, the television show. Anyway, my name is Andrew Johnson. I came to visit a friend, but it turns out she's got something to do."

Same old story... wait for it! Wait for it!

"Can I ask you out on a date?"

I shrugged. I wouldn't mind being asked out. It's been a while since someone did.

"Can I at least have a name?" he asked, his eyebrows rose expectantly. When I didn't respond, he continued. "You want me to make up one? I will. Okay then, Rebecca it is. No? Okay, Prue? Why am I not surprised? Fortunately, you can't read my mind right now."

I twitched my lips, raised my brows, shook my head, and shrugged.

He crossed his arm for a few seconds and then tucked his hands in his pockets, again.

"May I call you Phoebe? Simply because she is adventurous, and I'm hoping you are as well." He thinned his lips and looked into the brook below us. I took a sideways glance to see what he was looking at and saw a *few ducks glide over the rising tide and sighed.*

I didn't want it to seem like I was staring at him, and it was really hard not to, thus when he glanced at me, I averted my gaze. Why was I being difficult? He could be a player. But I was curious. It was cold and lonely, and I needed someone to talk to. I had gotten to the stage where books no longer bore solace, and fantasies were plain and no longer thrilling. I cautioned my heart and started walking away, reluctantly.

I was somewhat relieved that he blocked my path. My heart raced as my brain fought for control.

"I'm a bit hungry, so I'm hoping you can join me for dinner.

I wasn't sure if he was asking or telling, so I shrugged.

"You don't talk, do you?" he said in a syrupy voice.

I scoffed, suspecting I'd betrayed myself, but stayed mute.

For about an hour we scouted for an open restaurant. Finding none, we settled for Desperate Dan, a van that supplied food on the run, and decided on a chicken kebab. He talked for over an hour, and I enjoyed listening to his baritone voice. I was having such a nice time, and no cold wind could rain on my parade. Besides, it beat going back to the room to stare at the ceiling. I laughed so hard that my ribs hurt. Then at 10pm, the stupid alarm chimed from my phone.

He got up and clasped his hands behind him and turned to face me squarely. "I have a favour to ask of you, so... directly or indirectly?"

I tilted my head up, angling it to my left shoulder frowning, and narrowed my eyes at him. He must have cast a spell on me because I wanted to be with him and I had only just met him, in the park, at night, a mysterious, handsome face. It was the weekend, and with his looks, he should have a woman clinging to him.

"Can I have the privilege of tickling your pickle?"

My frown deepened. What on earth did he take me for? A looney? What did he even mean?

"Well, I have an offer. Please don't judge or shut me out..." he paused for a long time then said; "I want you to be my fuck buddy."

It felt like something hard and heavy had struck me. Was he expecting me to agree to that? Seriously? He wasn't ready for a proper relationship and didn't want any strings attached, but to think...

"I only wanted to see your reaction. What I really want, is, someone to pretend to be my girlfriend for three months, or maybe less, depending on when my mum heads back to the States. I will pay you handsomely if you agree, and I promise I will not touch you unless..." he smiled mischievously, "you want me to. Don't give me an answer now. Please think about it."

I questioned everything in me as I let him walk me home.

I pressed the buzzer to my friend's room when we arrived at the hostel. To break the silence, I said; "I had a nice time."

"Wow!" His voice boomed as his eyes widened. "You finally said something."

I heard the return buzz and pushed the door open and lingered. Still holding the door open but not letting him in.

"Why did you ask me that?" I asked hesitantly.

"I'm not sure. First, it was because we got along so well in no time and secondly, my mum will practically lick your fingers...sorry for the choice of words."

"Huh?"

"You are very beautiful..." he turned his head away slightly while scratching his ear then added, "and curved

in all the right places."

"Why did you ask me that?" I asked hesitantly.

"I'm not sure. First, it was because we got along so well in no time and secondly, my mum will practically lick your fingers...sorry for the choice of words."

"Huh?"

"You are very beautiful..." he turned his head away slightly while scratching his ear then added, "and curved in all the right places."

"How much?" I asked impatiently, trying to keep the desperation out of my voice.

"What?" he asked, blinking and frowning.

"How much will I be paid?"

"I will pay you ten thousand pounds a month whether she buys the story or not."

"Okay, there will be no sex, right?"

He nodded slowly.

"Then it's a deal! Goodnight!"

As soon as I shut the door, I hurried upstairs to my room and danced. Excitement conquered any chance of sleeping. I couldn't concentrate on the latest Men in Black movie I was streaming either, and it was hard to resist planning my expenses for when the money would arrive, even though I knew that it was bad to count your chickens before they hatched. I wondered if he had something else up his sleeve.

"Well, nothing ventured, nothing gained!" I said to myself. But I was restless. It was 4am and sleep still hadn't set in. I visited YouTube, played exercise videos and after thirty minutes of aerobics and one hour of dance exercise, I started feeling tired, but I had to fight slumber because I

had a doctor's appointment that morning, in less than an hour. Seeing that it was a losing battle, I quickly ran into the bathroom to take my bath. My well-planned list of expenses gradually changed as I stared at my teeth and face in the mirror. An hour later, as I appraised my reflection, I became a believer in cosmetic surgery and decided to browse the internet for the closest laser liposuction clinic in the area.

I had barely come out of the bathroom when I heard the buzzer. I rushed downstairs to answer the door. It was a parcel, and I signed for it. The delivery man said he was told to wait for my reply. I shrugged and quickly tore the wrapper. The gift was a brand-new smartphone with a note attached to it:

I didn't get your phone number or account number. Please call me on this number.
-Your Pretend Boyfriend.

Later that day, I checked my account and discovered it was in the black. I had more than enough money for the first time in forever. Suddenly, I was free from debt, except for my tuition, which would be taken care of in twenty-three days, ten hours, seventeen minutes and eleven seconds, when the next bill is scheduled to roll in. Right then, I had to get ready for my second date with my pretend boyfriend, Andrew. With my bandeau-enhanced bust in a little red dress, nothing could go wrong. I was still putting the final touches on my make-up when my phone started to ring. I ignored the first two times because it was from my ex-boyfriend.

Feeling wet and cold, I sat up abruptly. I blinked several times to bring my eyes to focus and squinted; the sun was up, and the sky clear. I followed the sound of giggling and rapid footsteps; children were on the footbridge throwing stones into the flowing water. I shook my head, disappointed that it was a dream. A few years ago, someone had said; a hungry person bore the most creative mind. Perhaps, that was true. How I wish this wasn't the case. It was such a good dream. I stretched on the bench I had slept on and inhaled deeply.

My stomach growled, but I chose to ignore it.

"This is going to be a long day," I moaned when it growled again. It's not like I had food in the house or any friend in town to *visit*.

My phone had rung a few times while I slept - it was my Dad. I prayed he would call back and decided to sit awhile and ponder on my almost realistic dream. It was so real I had to pinch my arm to remind me that it was only a dream.

My Dad had sent me £100. Fortune smiled on my bank instead because they had debited £96.66 and left me with only £6.74.

"Alas! Half bread is better than none! I better hurry before *Tesco* closes for the day."

Waterloo's Beast

Rotimi stared at the brown arch on his favourite shirt, a rainbow-striped designer shirt. His breath came in short gasps, his nose flared, his jaw and fists clenched. He didn't know what to do with Nneoma anymore. He was fed up, and the continuous corrections he'd issued her were beginning to drive him insane. It was like teaching a newborn to talk.

"Nneoma!" he shouted.

A scruffy woman ran into the corridor from the kitchen. She looked surreptitiously around. Everything seemed to be in place, but she still held her breath. "Yes, my good h-husband." she stammered, not looking him in the eye.

"What is this?" he asked, pointing at the shirt on the ironing board.

Her hands flew to her mouth and she fell to her knees, pleading. She'd been in a hurry to prepare his breakfast that she forgot to turn off the iron.

Can this woman get anything right? He thought as he glared at her then looked up at the time and hissed. *I will deal with this later.*

Nneoma heard her husband's shoes clap the floor she

had just polished. She shut her eyes tightly as it approached, her breath hitched when she felt he was close enough to strike her. Tension turned her body stiff and rigid.

Nothing happened.

She cautiously opened her eyes. He wasn't in front of her. She slanted her head in search of him and saw him climbing the stairs. She got up, fervently praying that he would dress up, go to work and forget the incident. Unsure, she chose to leave the house before he was done upstairs. So, to make him feel better and keep his fist to himself, she scurried in and out of the kitchen for a while. She set his food on the dining table then left a note near the tray.

Upstairs, Rotimi ground his teeth as he adjusted his tie. He tugged it off and looked for another one. He grimaced, the only organised place seemed to be his tie rack, even the gentle breeze from opening the wardrobe didn't have any effect.

He raised his brows as he studied his reflection. He was once told that a woman was the reflection of her husband; it was a lie he had believed. He shook his head and tugged off the second one. He was the poster boy for the organised and perceptive. But his wife?

On Monday, she gave me lumpy, pounded yam. Right after, she made my bathwater too hot. On Tuesday, she burnt the rice. I was in the sitting room, and I could smell it. Yet she was washing dishes beside the cooking pot and couldn't smell it? Wednesday, she burnt my camel-coloured chinos. Yesterday, she forgot to go to my mother's house, saying she had to get my laundry. She didn't even succeed in retrieving the so-called laundry. Today, she burns my designer shirt. The one I was to wear for my presentation.

What kind of wahala is this? Today of all days? I reject

this situation in Jesus Name! Amen! I don't need any more tongue wagging from that miserable spinster of a boss today. How could I, a deacon be married to an accursed woman such as this? She is so uncouth. Why didn't I notice this before? I prayed and fasted for a good woman... I'm in no position to question God but... hmm.

He called out to his wife, but she didn't answer. He walked purposefully to the kitchen, ready to pelt out the primitive behaviour that possessed her with his fists of discipline. On getting to the kitchen, he stumbled over a bucket of dirty water. Now irate, he yelled her name several times, then remembered he had asked her to go to the bank an hour ago.

He mumbled and accidentally kicked the bucket again spilling the dark water across the cream-coloured kitchen floor she had just finished mopping. He looked down at his beige chinos and groaned.

This woman will not be the death of me, in Jesus name. Amen.

Sunday mornings were noisy. The girls would bawl until their father came to their rescue. It always ended with Nneoma's head against the wall or his fist on her jaw. She would rather have him hit her head on the wall than her jaw against his fists because if he injured her jaw, he would take the children away and insist she stayed home. She had to go to church; it was the only social life she had.

The girls wanted her to do everything for them. If they had their way, what would they become? She needed them to be dependable and self-reliant. But since they were too young to understand what they were doing, she decided to wake them up two hours earlier. After they were dressed and had had their breakfast, she moved them to the sitting room and turned on the TV to distract them.

141

Nneoma looked at the time; she was going to be late if she didn't go to take her bath right away. She handed the remote control to Femi, her first child, and only son. She thanked God for giving her such a considerate child. He was the secret to her strength. She sighed as she looked back at him. He was too young for the responsibility he shouldered.

She quickly climbed the stairs. Looking over her shoulder at her husband's room, she heard water running, and assumed he was taking his bath. She ran to the children's room and turned on their shower. She had just finished lathering her skin with soap when she heard the shower curtain being pulled. Thinking it was one of the children; she stretched her hands over her body and asked who it was and what the problem was.

"What are you hiding?" Rotimi spat disdainfully.

"My good husband, good morning," she murmured and curtsied as she quickly washed her face.

"You have nothing worth hiding," he continued, disgust smothering his face. "You are as fat as a pig. You have the house all to yourself, and you can't make out time to exercise to lose all that weight?" He grimaced as he gestured.

"I'm sorry," she retorted and curtsied again.

"Sorry for yourself. Where are my clothes?"

She scrambled to get out of the bath. "Let me get them for you."

"Forget it. Just get ready." He gave her a long condescending gaze and left the bathroom.

She quickly showered and was soon ready and waiting for him downstairs with the children. When he came down, he took a long look at her and said; "I'll go with the kids. You find your own way."

She waited for him to leave. As soon as he was left, she went to the kitchen window and looked out. Bartholomew, their neighbour's car was still parked behind their building.

Hoping to hitch a ride to church, she called to him. They attended the same church. She just had to insist that he drops her off on the street before the one the church was on. Then, from there, she would take the short cut by the old woman's house beside the church.

Bartholomew looked around, frowned then looked up, surprised.

She gestured, and he waited. She went to get her Bible and dashed to the door to make her exit. It was locked. She went to the bureau, but her keys were not there. It was the only place she had ever kept her keys. She opened the lowest drawer in search of the bunch of spare keys but didn't find them either. She rushed to the kitchen, but it was also locked.

She blinked back the tears that were threatening to ruin her make-up. Her legs felt wobbly, and she sank to the ground leaning on the kitchen door. Someone knocked on the kitchen door, the jangling keys assured her it was Bartholomew, but she didn't want to answer the door. How could she tell anyone that her husband had locked her in? Besides, if he knew her husband had locked her in, he'll break the door and possibly inform her sister, and her bruises will only multiply.

Later that day, when Rotimi got home from church, he reminisced on the good he had done the week before, as they were told to do in church. He sat at his reading table with a pen in hand as he tapped his chin.

On Monday morning on his way to work, he heard a few squabbles; it was a common trend in the compound, so he didn't want to concern himself with any of it. As he walked towards the gate, he saw Abdullahi's hand around his wife's neck, her arms and legs flailing. He averted his gaze and pretended to have a phone call as he left. A tenant in the building heading off to work shouted at Abdullahi's wife, "You sef shut up! You want him to kill you before you close your mouth?"

"Tell her o! Like mother, like daughter!" Abdullahi retorted through clenched teeth.

"Kill her o! Thank God sey she never born pikin for am," a tenant from the flat upstairs shouted.

Another tenant tugging her children in faded school uniforms bellowed, "You sef comot for road. Some of us have somewhere to go."

The girl in youth service garbs stepped out of the way. A lady asking for directions also shrunk away from the gate. And the woman pushed the children out before stepping out through the gate herself.

Abdullahi, exhausted, let go of his wife. She sprung to her feet and started raining abuses on him. He shook his head slowly the first time she hit him, but after the second one, he pounced on her. He wrapped his arms around her waist, and she grabbed his legs. He fell backwards and she landed on him. He remained motionless for a while. He was a tall frail-looking man and his wife... well, he was only a tenth the size of her. She remained on top of him, and the students from a university that was on strike looked down from their balcony, taking pictures of them. Abdullahi pleaded, but she insisted on an apology. After a while, he surrendered, and she got off him.

As soon as she got off him, he pushed her towards the house, pulled out his koboko, wrapped his legs around hers, and began to flog her. She screamed, but no one came, probably because it was a Monday morning or because they were notorious for being a nuisance.

He returned because he'd forgotten a file at home and caught Abdullahi flogging his wife.

"Stop that this instant," Rotimi ordered.

Abdullahi continued to flog his wife.

Rotimi grabbed Abdullahi's hand firmly. "How dare you hit a woman?"

"Oga, Sir, you know not this woman, what trouble she is."

"If she is so much trouble, why are you still with her?"

"No money to send her back to people."

"Ehen, so you want to discard her now after you have enjoyed her, abi?"

Abdullahi frowned, his head low and murmured, "Oga, Sir, is because is you o!"

"Shut up! If her father finds out you beat her, do you know what will happen to you?"

Abdullahi covered his mouth then bit his finger.

Rotimi gestured to Abdullahi, who nodded and walked to where his wife sat sobbing and rocking herself.

The ringtone of his phone disconnected him from his thoughts. A few seconds after peering at it, he started typing his advice to his cousin's wife. The new bride was asking for his help because her husband had started hitting her. He spent a few more minutes texting her before going back to the assignment he'd been working on.

On Wednesday, he discovered that he was out of shaving sticks. He decided to go to the Aboki's kiosk at the end of the road. On his way there, he saw a man beating a child with a large plank. He stopped the man from beating the child and cussed the man. The man stood with arms akimbo, looking amused. After a while, he paused, irritated by the man's attitude.

"You think I'm funny, abi?"

"No, I think you should learn to mind your business."

"You want to kill her because she is not your child."

The man smirked. "Do you know her father?"

"No, but that's beside the point. You have no -"

"I'm her father." The man said so calmly that Rotimi was taken aback.

"So what? If you kill her, then what? You don't have a womb, you know. You don't know what it takes."

A woman came out of nowhere. "Ehen, your fellow man has told you to stop too. Kill her and wait for me to bear you another one, you hear!"

He left them arguing because he was going to be late for fellowship. He still had issues with the church moving the fellowship from Tuesdays to Wednesdays, which he usually spent with the boys at Dingy Den.

He was still writing down his good deeds of the past week

when he heard the doorbell. He didn't come out of his study but listened in.

"Oh, pastor, welcome!" Nneoma said as she stepped back to let her friend in.

"You know I don't like it when you call me pastor. I'm a pastor's wife, not a pastor."

"Ihinòse," Nneoma said, chuckling. "You're a pastor in the making."

The children were upstairs taking their siesta, so there was no one else in the sitting room. Ihinòse looked around while Nneoma went to get refreshments. As soon as Nneoma came out, Ihinòse asked in a loud whisper. "Where is your husband?"

Nneoma chuckled gesturing with the tray in her hands. "Come over here *jò*!"

Ihinòse sat down at the edge of one of the sofas for a few seconds before sliding into it. "Where is your husband?" she asked again with a serious look on her face.

"Taking a nap, I think."

"And you?"

Nneoma shrugged and turned on the TV.

"Girl, you need to get out more," Ihinòse mumbled.

"Hmm?"

Ihinòse shook her head and took a long sip of the juice Nneoma had offered her. "I'll never advise you to leave your husband's house as a pastor's wife. But girl, you're no chicken. He has already plucked every feather and left you naked, so you might as well..." she blurted and looked away, "walk out."

"I have kids with him," Nneoma replied in staccato, her eyes threatening to bulge out of their sockets.

"So?"

"They need their mother," she murmured, looking at her

feet.

"Their mother?" Ihinòse spun glaring at her friend. "Where is she? Because she is not who I see."

"Stop it, *nawh*." Nneoma let out a mirthless chuckle and playfully nudged her friend.

Ihinòse glared at her friend. "You think this is funny, *abi*? Don't worry. Were we not in the same class as the Osaki twins? Don't worry that is your portion."

"God forbid!" Nneoma said, rising and glaring at her friend simultaneously.

Ihinòse ignored her. "You know the despicable things she made those kids do at an early age. The men that carried them off in big cars and brought them back in the morning a few hours before school resumed. That is what will happen to your daughters if you continue to stay."

Nneoma was already panting and pointing a shaky finger at the door. "Leave."

"I will!" Ihinòse had already placed her bag on her shoulder. "I will go. Your husband uses you as a punching bag, which is where you are supposed to show your power, my dear. It's obvious you don't want your children to have a mother. Me, I have said my piece. After all, advice *no be* curse. I'm talking to you as a friend, so I have cleared my conscience."

Nneoma shut the door on her friend, who was still talking. She couldn't care; she had to prepare her husband's food so that it would be ready as soon as he woke up. She hoped he would be okay with fish, as he hadn't yet given her money to go shopping. She liked fish, but she was willing to sacrifice it for him. He deserved it. The kids were going to their grandmother's house for the midterm holiday. She was going to give him a manicure and pedicure before dinner then massage his feet right after, just like he liked it. That would calm him.

She hoped and prayed it would be enough.

Rotimi punched a fist into his other palm. If she hadn't sent the witch who called herself a pastor's wife away, he would have kicked the woman out himself and dealt with Nneoma immediately after. Anyway, forgiveness was what they were taught today. It was Sunday after all!

He conveniently forgot the fact that he had pushed her off the bed on Monday morning to prepare his food when she had just gone to bed two hours before because he wanted to eat *moi-moi* in the morning, and he had only informed her at midnight. On Tuesday, he tipped the *egusi* soup on her head because there wasn't enough seasoning and then beat her. He went to visit his mother on Wednesday and didn't return until Friday evening. He beat her for not asking him how his day went and accused her of bringing a man home while he was away, then raped her after which he forced her to sleep on the concrete floor.

Or even the fact that since they became man and wife, he tut-tutted whenever she had an opinion. He had a doctorate, and she had just a WAEC, so what could she proffer? He had made it a point of duty to snuff out any furore she might still hold.

A few weeks had passed. He was now on holiday. While he was listening to the news that morning, he heard a knock. Puzzled, he went to answer the door and found Bartholomew there, grinning, and frowned.

Bartholomew cleared his throat and craned his neck to look behind Rotimi.

Rotimi snickered and smirked.

"Mr Adelaja, I have these bags for your wife."

Rotimi grimaced, crossed his arms, and leaned on the door. "From you, I presume."

149

Bartholomew shrugged. "I met your wife's sister yesterday, and she asked me to give these to your wife. I couldn't come yesterday as I arrived very late."

Rotimi eyed him and stretched his hand out. "I see."

Bartholomew stared at him, looking confused.

"The bags," he retorted with contempt.

"Oh!" Bartholomew handed them over and walked away briskly.

Rotimi retreated and kicked the door shut. He dumped the bags on the floor, carefully folded the sleeves of his shirt, then went in search of Nneoma. He was still angry that she had smiled at a man who winked at her when they escorted his cousin to the bus stop an hour ago. He didn't want her to join them in the first place, but his cousin had insisted. She even led the cousin to believe that he was beating her. Imagine that!

"Nneoma!" he shouted at the top of his voice.

She scurried into the sitting room and curtsied, her head low.

"Why do you keep on disgracing me?"

Nneoma swallowed. *I didn't leave any of his clothes outside, I hope.* She scanned her mind for something she may have forgotten to do but didn't come up with anything.

"Look at this woman o! Am I talking to myself?"

"But -" She never got to finish her sentence because her ear began to ring. She covered it and looked up to see where she needed to protect next, but it was too late, her other ear had started to ring too. The clanging cymbals in her ear seemed to shift its echo to her forehead.

She knew how much he hated it when her hands came up. She was supposed to act like a good child taking corrections. But she couldn't help it. Her hands wouldn't stay down at the jolt of pain. Her body would cringe at any pain in her stomach even before it happened. He rarely ever hit her in the face, which meant he was furious.

Rotimi mumbled his irritation. He had shown and taught her everything; how to behave, talk, and even when to smile. What to wear and how to wear it. Only whores wore short dresses, miniskirts, and body-hugging dresses. She had learnt well. He had taught her how to serve his food; she took that well. He had rationed her visits and letter-tossing between family and friends, and she had taken that well. Why then would her twin sister be sending her things if they weren't in touch?

He pulled her by the ear towards the centre of the room. He didn't notice that there was a stool in front of him until he toppled over it with her. Infuriated, he kicked her, but she had guarded her stomach, so his feet came in contact with her knee. Hurt, he lashed out, slapping her all over, especially on her back. She remained curled up like a foetus.

She would protect her ribs; that was where her heart and breath were. The last time, he broke her ribs, the doctor told her parents, who in turn told his parents, who in turn told him, and that only made things worse. Bartholomew had a chemist, and she already owed him a lot of money.

Men were horrible, Rotimi had said, she couldn't work. The children had three square meals, and she was supposed to remain slim and eat only when he told her to. It was difficult before, but she was now used to it. She would not offend him any further, not with the children being more observant nowadays. No man likes to sit at home when his children need care and protection. He must be frustrated being at home. She would make him *moi-moi*, his favourite.

She began to feel numb all over and wondered if she'd remembered to eat as the light went out of her eyes.

"The children will be going to their grandmother's today.

Just get what they will need," he muttered, paused, took a long look at her. "The driver will drop them off."

"Yes, my good husband," she retorted and curtsied.

"Daddy, good morning," the children chorused. They huddled around him, ready to be driven to school. He dropped them on Wednesdays.

"My angels, I can't drop you off today."

"But daddy," Femi murmured sourly.

"No, your mother will drop you off," he said and went back inside, not bothering to give Femi a hug. The twin girls were in his way; he lifted them and set them aside.

Nneoma rushed back inside to get her car keys.

Femi nudged his younger sister, Omolayo, out of his way.

"Why does Daddy beat Mummy?" Omolayo asked.

Nneoma was coming out when she overheard her son and froze.

Omolayo frowned. "Daddy doesn't beat Mummy, he disciplines her."

"No, he doesn't," Shade, one of the twins, said in a loud whisper. "He beats her so she doesn't run away."

"Why would she run away?" Olamide asked.

"Will she leave us?" Mayowa asked, looking worried.

"No, she will never leave us. Now, enough questions." Femi sighed exasperatedly and said under his breath, "I hope he doesn't kill her like Zainab's father killed her mother." He thought of what his best friend was going through and shuddered.

Nneoma froze when she heard her son's words. She hadn't realised that her children knew. She jingled her keys.

Olamide jumped and grumbled, "Mummy, you scared me o!"

"Oh, sorry, my dear, I didn't mean to."

Femi frowned and relaxed. She must not have heard a thing or she would have asked him twenty-one-questions.

Nneoma dropped the children off at school and quickly drove back home to finish her chores. She parked the car and was about to step out when something caught her eye. She looked again. Unsure, she picked it up. It was lipstick. She didn't wear lipstick. It dawned on her that it was her husband's car. Quickly, she climbed out, locked it, and ran inside to replace the key before he'd discover what she had done. Besides, she was still sore from the last reprimand. She ran up the stairs ignoring the sound from the TV and went headlong into the room before she realised that the moaning sound wasn't from the TV downstairs, but from the woman her husband was mating with. She remained on the spot, unsure of what to do. She couldn't think, so she left the room and closed the door behind her.

She leaned on the door and then slid to the ground, hugging herself. Rotimi hadn't touched her in years, except twice the past weeks when he raped her. Not that it bothered her anymore, but seeing him on another woman stirred in her, something she had long forgotten. Now she remembered what the stirring was; it was desire. When was the last time she had felt that way?

It was at her niece, Chikodi's dedication, a long time ago. She remembered it clearly; Femi had an unsteady bowel release, so potty training was on-going, even though his younger sisters had long stopped wearing disposable napkins. They were heading towards the front of the church when the smell followed her husband. He wrinkled his nose and glared at his wife. Nneoma took Femi to the toilet, but there was no water to wash him with. She remembered she had to buy *pure* water from a kiosk almost a mile away because it was Sunday. Relying on the fact that Femi wouldn't poop until they got home, she didn't bother to carry extra clothing.

That was the day the beatings started. Because she had

disobeyed him, she had inevitably disgraced him. She had longed for his touch all day, and he rewarded her with a beating that stifled any longing she had had for him, until now. She swallowed saliva to lubricate her throat.

Nine years on, I have endured everything, and then he brings another woman to our home. How can I be longing for a beast who masquerades himself as a man? O, God! I dug for myself a grave with my eyes wide open. How could I not have seen this coming? I have been oblivious to the nature of the beast as he courted me. How?

She chewed the insides of her cheek.

Will this be the distraction that keeps him away from me until I have nursed myself back to health? My entire being needs urgent recovery. The pummelling has been on the increase since he lost his job two weeks ago; there is only so much my body can take.

Nneoma roused herself and started to walk towards her son's room when she heard Rotimi say, "My wife doesn't know how to give it to me as well as you do." She shrugged; it would be the miracle she needed to keep his fists from getting a release on her already battered skin.

"That is why I'm your Yemisi *nawh!*" the woman drawled.

Nneoma sniggered.

"I know, I know, let me rest small before we do it again." Rotimi murmured.

Nneoma cupped her chest as she dreaded hearing him saying the sweet things he used to say to her during lovemaking to another woman.

"That is what you always say, but you're not taking care of me well." She heard the woman say.

Yes, that is my husband, selfish as always.

"*Haba*, have I not been crediting your account?"

Nneoma halted and started retracing her steps back to

154

the spot she had just left.

A brief silence ensued.

"And paid your children's fees?" Rotimi's voice increased a tad.

Nneoma's eyes threatened to fall out of its sockets. She shook her head, disagreeing with what she'd heard.

Another brief silence.

"Even that store you wanted, didn't I rent and stock it up for you?"

And yet another brief silence.

Nneoma covered her mouth. She didn't know why she did that probably because she didn't want to waken the beast in him or preventing herself from screaming in shock as her heart urged her to choke the life out of him. The past year her parents had been the ones paying the children's fees, indirectly of course. His whore can run a business, and she couldn't?

"Now be a good woman and take care of this man," Rotimi groaned.

The woman chuckled. "Let me rest a little, and then I'll make you cry like a baby Oliver Twist."

"With a *bakassi* like yours, I will cry well well."

"I thought you said you had a housewife, where is she?"

"That trash I picked from the gutter?" He smirked. "She went to drop my children at school."

"But she will come back very soon. Ha! I don't want trouble o!"

"She cannot bamboozle you from my bosom. Relax, I'm the man of this house!"

Nneoma felt dizzy and held the wall for support. The walls around the corridor felt like they were caving in on her and shut her eyes for a few seconds. She bit the inside of her cheek fervently, her stomach felt like it was carrying a large stone, her skin had begun to itch, and her ears felt hot. She pulled her knees to herself and rested her chin on them to feel grounded, but she started shivering.

When Rotimi started telling the woman words that were supposed to be said to her, her mind urged her to cover her ears, but her heart was so eager to hear those words that she had longed to hear for almost a decade. She could hear him grunt like a raging bull and the woman begging for more. It was a matter of time before her husband will head for round three; nothing was complete unless it was in threes with him.

She needed to leave. Although her body shook violently and she could hear her teeth clatter, she remained frozen to the spot. She couldn't be cold, it was past midday in the middle of harmattan season, and besides, she was sweating. She didn't know how long she had been in that position, but it was quiet. It was too quiet. It took her a while to realise that her blurry vision was caused by her tears. Her body was no longer shaking but numb.

She dragged herself towards the stairs. She didn't know what came over her except that she felt an unusual calm. Her lips were moving to words she knew well but didn't remember how. She knew the beautiful voice was hers, but it sounded distant, like an echo.

When she got downstairs, her body dragged her towards the kitchen. She was done tidying the kitchen. She urged her brain to take her upstairs, but her body wasn't responding to her. It felt devoid of pain, so she decided to enjoy her freedom from pain. She was beginning to like this macho part of her and wondered where it had been hiding all this while.

She leaned on the kitchen door frame with arms across her body as she tapped on her chin. She smiled through singing, then leaned over the sink and turned on the tap. She pulled an aluminium basin from under the sink and kept it on the worktop. She produced a pair of scissors from the cabinet and placed it gently beside the basin then went into the pantry and came back with all the bags of pepper. Rocking herself, she turned on the blender and poured the ungrounded pepper into it. While the blender crushed its little red victim, she emptied the grounded ones into the basin.

Her eyes watered each time she sneezed.

Exasperated, she glared at her hands then stroked them tenderly. Morose and eager, she scratched her head, trying to remember something and raised a finger then applauded for herself. She went to the shelves beside the door leading to the pantry and opened the first aid kit and stared derisively at it for a while.

Finally, she took out a pair of gloves, emptied the rest of the contents into a cellophane bag which she stashed in the washing bucket under the sink then pulled the gloves on. As an afterthought pulled on another set of gloves and tapped a small bowl. Smiling complacently, Nneoma emptied the blender into the basin and carried the basin upstairs, singing. When she got to the landing, she heard him groan like a laboured cow and giggled.

Using her big buttocks, she pushed their bedroom door open. Rotimi didn't hear her come in because he was still fondling the woman. They both lay sprawled on the bed, exhausted from their feat. Nneoma padded softly towards them; she was at the edge of the bed before they noticed her. Before Rotimi could say anything, Nneoma had tossed two bowlfuls of pepper on him in quick succession before using her hands to toss it like it was confetti.

Yemisi tried to cover her private parts, but it was too late. Yemisi screamed and cursed, Rotimi yelped like a hungry puppy. Nneoma giggled; he did like his pepper hot.

Rotimi scrambled off the bed, groping around. Noticing

he was heading to the bathroom; she pulled a chair from under the dressing table and placed it on his path. For good measure, she doused the entire bathroom with her red dust of vengeance and garnished the towels too then walked out, not forgetting to shut the door behind her. She hopped down the stairs, still singing, *My Favourite Things* from The Sound of Music.

She clapped her hands gleefully when she remembered that it was his shaving day, so she tapped her feet to the tune she sang as she pondered her next course of action. She bent down to retrieve the methylated spirit from the bag she had stashed under the sink and went back to the bedroom, stealthily opened the door, meandered around her husband and went into the bathroom, emptied half of the husband's aftershave, filled it with methylated spirits, she shook it for good measure and walked around him then continued her singing.

Yemisi pleaded.

Nneoma looked at her for a while, not finding her interesting, hummed and continued towards the door and was about to close it when the intruding woman called her a witch. She tilted her head, smiling gleefully as she stopped mid-stride and pivoted. She pulled the woman's hand gently, but the woman shoved her off and started shouting for help. She walked around the woman and tugged her off the bed, then began to drag her out of the room by the hair. Halfway out of the room, she remembered her husband's phones, went back into the room, and took them. Her eyes fell on his laptop, and she picked it up too. She went to the balcony of the children's sitting room upstairs. With her hands over the railings, she let go.

Someone shouted, "Who *be* that?"

Oblivious, Nneoma was back to where she had left the woman who had groped her way to the stairs. Nneoma sniggered. Grinning at the convenience, she dragged Yemisi down the stairs, opened the door, and pushed her out. Soon after she shut the door, she tapped her chin as she considered her next line of action.

She returned to the pantry and brought out all the petroleum jelly stored there and scooped the content into a pot. As soon as it melted, she carried the large basin upstairs. Rotimi was no longer in bed, his eyes were still closed as he sat underneath the shower. She nodded her approval when she saw him in the bath.

She stared at the floor and nodded to herself. *Tile is always better*. She removed all the mats in the bathroom and poured the greasy liquid on the floor. He tried to grab her, but she was far from his reach, and he didn't want to get out from under the soothing torrents of water. Not long after, she heard a thud, then another and smiled. She joyfully returned to the room and saw him on the floor in the bathroom, trying to get up and left.

Rotimi finally got up and limped out of the bathroom. He got into a pair of beach shorts and singlet and picked up his car keys. When he got to the hallway, he found Nneoma humming, her arms wrapped around a basket full of laundry. He walked menacingly towards her. He raised a hand at her and missed her by a smidgen; she had turned to unhook one of the clothes from the doorknob. He lost his balance and used his injured leg to stop himself from falling. The shock of the pain caused him to lift his injured leg. He stumbled and toppled down the stairs but still able to shield his head.

Nneoma stopped tugging the cloth to listen for the sound and shrugged. *The noise must have come from outside*. She folded the children's clothes and sorted the ones they'd be wearing to their grandmother's and a few more. After sorting her husband's clothes, she came back to their bedroom and discovered that Rotimi was not there.

Nneoma sighed her relief. *He would keep his whores out of this house from now on*. She twisted her mouth at the mess she'd made. *This room needs cleaning*. She wrapped the blanket and pillows with the bed sheet until it looked like an onion bulb, tossed it at the stairs, then proceeded to wash the bathroom, prepare lunch for Rotimi in case he came back feeling hungry.

She heard the honk of a horn and bounded downstairs with a travelling bag filled with the children's clothes. She opened the door just as the driver was about to knock. He took the bag from her and nodded his thanks. She threw her arms around her children, but they quickly untangled themselves and hurried up the stairs to get changed. A few minutes later, they huddled around her and she kissed them and waved them goodbye.

Finishing her chores, she took her bath and came downstairs to watch a rerun when she saw Rotimi's cousin, the wife, and his elder brother. She wasn't away for that long then it hit her; Rotimi had gone to get his relatives. She greeted them; they greeted her and quickly left.

Where could they be heading off to in such a hurry?

Meanwhile, Rotimi pretended to be asleep on the settee. She was surprised to see his face scrunched up.

She watched an episode of *Secrets of the Sand*. Bored and restless, she went into the kitchen looking for what to do and settled for making another batch of her husband's favourite; *moi moi*.

Nneoma washed and soaked the beans then entered the sitting room to turn off the light. She found her husband still sleeping; she tapped her chin, pondering. She waltzed into the kitchen, soaked grounded crayfish and applied it to the sole of his foot that wasn't in a cast then left the kitchen door open. That night rats feasted on the foot.

The plaster of Paris on one foot didn't prevent Rotimi from trying to beat her. He succeeded in kicking her on the shin and grunted. Nneoma didn't wince or react in any way except that she picked up the pestle and swung it. It collided with his head, and he went flat onto the ground.

His head reeled for a few minutes before he recognised his environment. *She must have soddened the carpet*, he thought because it felt wet. His head throbbed, his stomach groaned, his bladder wanted release. He was also desperately thirsty, and his vision shadowy.

The air conditioning isn't supposed to be on, he thought and tried to raise himself to go turn it off but couldn't lift his weight. *I should have taken the doctor's advice*; *'make sure you eat before you drink these'.*

He muttered his wife's name, but she didn't answer. *Why is she ignoring me? No problem, as soon as I sleep this headache off, she will learn.* He murmured her name again. *Where does her mind sail off to? Is there another man? No, Abdullahi would have informed me.*

Nneoma returned to the living room and peered at him, wondering why he was opening and closing his mouth. Anyway, she had something more important to do; she had forgotten to wash her children's bathroom. *When he gets over his laziness he would get up and stop making a nuisance of himself*, she thought as she continued cleaning and tidying.

Rotimi murmured again. After a while, he saw her approach him and was glad that she was no longer ignoring him. He called out to her again.

Nneoma hovered around him with her washing bucket as she tried to figure out when he started moaning in his sleep.

161

Rotimi frowned at the figure he suspected was his wife and called out again.

With arms akimbo and raised brows, she bent over him. Seeing the spill on the ground near his head, she frowned and touched it. It was red and smelt metallic.

"Why are you pretending not to hear me?" Rotimi hissed, glared at her and blinked. *It is blood, you idiot; it is blood, my blood. Oh dear, I'm bleeding. That cannot be good o!* Alarmed, he gestured as he ordered her to get the doctor. *She is obstinate, this woman. I'm bleeding and she just looking at my blood on her hands! What is wrong with this woman? Why is she smiling like a fool? And what is that stupid song she has been humming?*

Her brows furrowed as she wondered why and when barbeque sauce was spilled. Knowing what Rotimi was like, she decided to clean it up before he woke up.

Rotimi apologised and pleaded with her to lift him up as she hovered around him, her eyes glassy and distant. He tried to figure out what she was singing as he passed out.

Jane's Vibe

Jane saw her husband, Tobias, step out of a taxi and frowned. The taxi should have parked on their cobbled driveway. It was a busy road, and he wasn't a very careful person.

Tobias jumped when a red Audi swerved past him and lost his footing. Fortunately, he landed on the grass on their side of the road. There was a screech of tyres as the car came to a halt and a woman with long red hair ran towards her husband. Jane leaned on the railing of the balcony to observe but couldn't see anything because of the woman bent over him. The red-haired woman stood up with a hand on her hip and the other, making circles in the air.

Jane twisted her mouth; the woman was taking too long, and she couldn't make out who she was from the balcony. Agitated, she pressed the bell forcefully. The maid ran towards her, stopping with a shrill sound produced by her white plimsolls on the marble floor.

"Ma'am?" the maid queried while trying to catch her breath.

"Quickly, go and find out who that woman is," Jane answered, pointing in the direction of her husband's fall.

A few moments later, Tobias was at the door.

"Are you alright?" he asked when he saw the maid slide down the banister.

The maid brushed past him.

He shrugged, hung his coat in the cloakroom and loosened his tie as he trotted up the stairs. Soon after he got into his bedroom, he picked up the remote control to turn on the TV and called out to his wife simultaneously then increased the volume of the TV, pressed the information button of the remote control, laughing, and threw it on the bed.

Carry on up the jungle, yeah! He picked up the remote control again and pressed the record button before going to the balcony in search of his wife. While he unbuttoned his shirt, he followed his wife's gaze, but only saw a little boy on skates with a dog galloping after him. Smiling, he nuzzled his wife's neck and said, "You are positively agog about something."

The maid reappeared, looking a little dishevelled and panting. Jane signalled her to say nothing.

"Is there anything else you need, Ma'am?" the maid asked, almost failing to hide her contempt.

"No, that will be all. You may retire for the night."

The maid nodded. "Good night, Sir, Ma'am."

"Good night, Felicity," Tobias muttered, nodding absentmindedly.

Jane waved her away.

"How was your day?" Jane asked Tobias once she heard the slam of the door downstairs.

"Okay."

"Really? Because you sound like you are bursting to tell me something," she urged a little too eagerly, as she deftly wrapped the blanket around her legs.

"I got a new project which will set us up for a long time and knock down all our bills..."

Blah blah blah... She had already zoned out. Her keen interest was finding out who the woman was and why she had been hovering over him. *Who was that bitch? Who was she? WHO WAS THAT WOMAN FOR GOODNESS' SAKE?* "Who was that red-head?"

He arched his brow, wearing a mischievous smile.

She crossed her arm and asked in a serious tone. "Who was that woman?"

"Oh! That was Belinda."

Jane's eyes looked like they were going to pop out of their sockets and Tobias laughed. She gritted her teeth and pulled her afro until it hurt. Her nemesis and he seemed to be taking the piss.

The same red-haired girl who had made her a spectacle throughout sixth form. The girl who had put peanuts in her scrambled egg so that she would be a mess of herself on her hen night; being allergic, her face was double its size and looked like a large potato. That same girl that tied the belt of her dress to a curtain on her first meeting with Tobias' parents, and laughed at her when she tripped and fell, taking the curtain down with her and exposing Elton, her soon-to-be mother-in-law's twin in a compromising position with the hired male bartender. His stoic wife has since not spoken to her.

What did she want this time? To ridicule me because I'm now in a wheelchair? Tobias never sees things my way. How can he be taking sides with her already?

Irritated, Jane stretched her hand to the half-empty bottle of wine on the dining table. Groaning because she couldn't reach it, she instead brushed the empty ones out of the way.

Tobias was woken by a whistling sound which was followed by a crashing sound. He only raced down the stairs when he realized his wife wasn't beside him. She was by the sink, and there were shards of ceramic and glass around her feet, but she wasn't wounded, *unfortunately*.

Leaning on the wall, he crossed his arms, pondering the wisdom of assisting her. Then, he caught a glimpse of an empty bottle lying on the counter. He moved closer and saw more bottles.

He grimaced and scrubbed his face. *This is the fifteenth bottle in one week. If she keeps this up, there'll be nothing left of my small, overpriced wine cellar.*

He looked down at her, turned her around to face him. She was sobbing and smelled of alcohol. Her hands were shaking when he took them in his so he drew her into an embrace, wiping her already red and puffy face and said, "You can't go on like this, you know. It's gonna' be alright."

She shoved him off. "Leave me alone!"

"Well, I can't!"

"Fuck off!" she yelled, running into his shin as she reversed her wheelchair.

Tobias gritted his teeth and nursed his shin.

"Just go and meet her. You think I don't know about you and Belinda? Just because I'm in a wheelchair, you've decided to go gallivanting ..."

"Gallivanting?" he asked, astounded, still rubbing his shin. It wasn't the first time she had accused him of cheating on her. In the past, three years ago to be almost precise, she would often come to the office unannounced to catch him out. It was little wonder that she never made a scene. But since the accident a year and four months ago, it has become a petition. He was getting rather sick of it.

"You've been cheating on me," she agreed with herself.

He let out an exasperated sigh with outstretched arms. "Come on, love ..."

"Love? *Love*? You must think I'm stupid. Those women's cheap perfumes escort you home every day." She rolled her chair to the sitting room, unscrewed the lid of a half-full bottle of rum and took a swig.

"Love..." she scoffed and then rolled her chair towards the staircase. She hit it several times, trying to set her chair right in front of the stairs. She gave him a long condescending look. "You can at least help me up the stairs."

"JANE!"

Startled by his voice, she turned her head to face him.

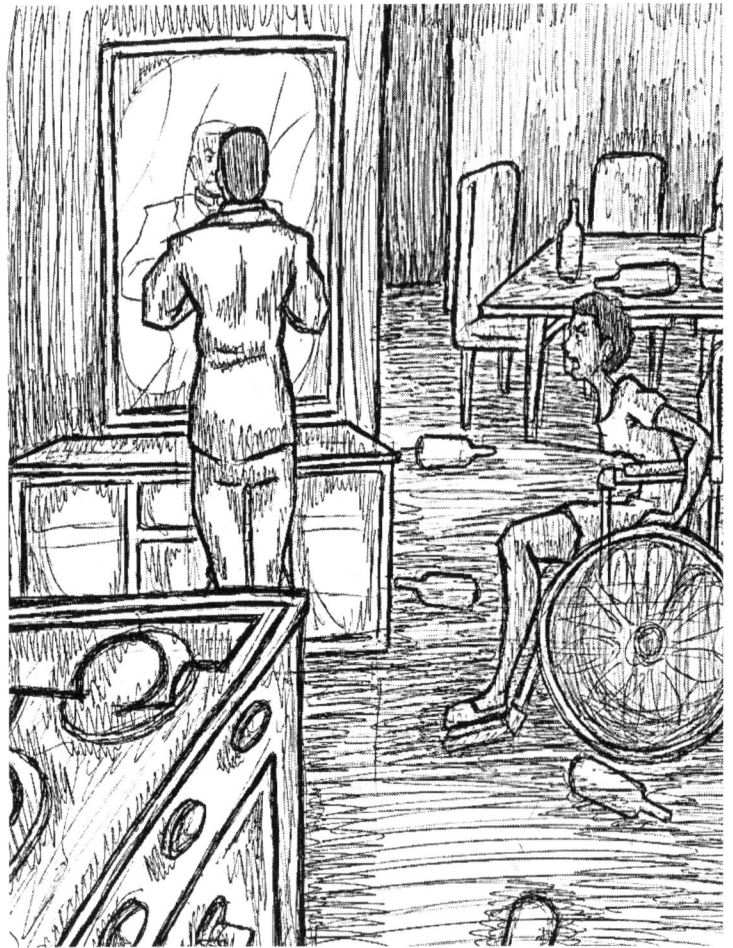

"I have had enough of your childish outbursts of bad temper. Why don't you pour your anger into something more useful, like being my wife or getting out of that fucking chair, rather than blame the world for your...." he exhaled heavily as he stroked his tousled hair back in place. "For the past year-plus, you've been a roller coaster of emotions. It baffles me that you still have tears to spare. I'm tired of these fights, for goodness' sake!"

She bit her lip and started sulking.

He shook his head. "Fine. Let's get one thing straight, though. I'm not having an affair." He paused for a while. "Now, let me take you -."

"Don't touch me," she shrieked and moved away from him as if something hot had scalded her. He ignored her and carried her upstairs.

Two hours later, they were back in the kitchen where he made toast and omelettes; except in his own, there were chives. He watched her eye the jar of raspberry jam that was a few inches above her. She started fidgeting and gave him a slanted look. He looked back at his food before she could catch him watching.

She was sure he wasn't looking but carried it off the counter successfully. Placing it between her thighs, she wheeled herself into the space created for her at the dining table. As soon as they finished eating, the bell rang, and he threw down his napkin, picked up his briefcase, and went to answer the door, but not before he blew her a perfunctory kiss.

"Hi!" her nurse and maid chorused their greeting.

Jane gritted her teeth in reply - they served to remind her of her predicament.

At work, Tobias idly fidgeted with a pencil when the ringing phone pierced through his thoughts. Reluctantly, he picked it up.

"Dr Manning, you've got a call on line three."

"Patch it through." He murmured and waited for the clicking sound. "Hello?"

"Please don't cut this call. I need to speak with you urgently," the voice at the other end stammered softly.

"What do you want, Belinda?" Tobias asked,

uncomfortably

"I need your help," she retorted.

"You haven't answered my question."

"I -"

"And I haven't got all day," he said, fiddling with his tie. He could tell she was toying her curly hair and he smiled. She always did that when she was thinking of what to say. He wasn't sure of what he felt for her. Initially, he thought it was a crush, but it felt more like an obsession. She wasn't hot, but she had grey eyes with specks of violet in them. He

loved those eyes and had at one time wished all girls had them.

It wouldn't hurt to meet for coffee, would it?

"Please, can we meet?" she asked, sounding sincere. "Let's meet and I'll explain."

There was a brief silence.

"Fine," he conceded.

"Dinner, say eight o'clock?"

Yeah right! "Lunch."

"Okay."

"Where?"

"There's a new restaurant on Nelson Street…" she trailed off.

He could tell she was smiling. *Going to a new restaurant with another woman? In this little town? Fat chance!*

"Prego's will do," he sighed. Tilting his head to see the time, he added. "in an hour."

Readjusting his tie, he waited impatiently for a few clients checking his watch for the umpteenth time within the same minute.

Two hours later he went to Prego's. He had taken a secluded spot in the second room of the restaurant. He glanced around uncomfortably. It looked like a romantic setting. He wouldn't want Belinda or anyone else that may know him, to get the wrong idea. He could have left an hour ago, but he wanted to see her again. He was tapping away on his phone and only glanced up when he heard a chair scrape the floor.

"Hi! Sorry, I'm late," Belinda said quickly as she hung her jacket behind the chair and dramatically slid into her chair.

He got up abruptly to push her chair in.

Belinda didn't make an effort to hide her flirtatious gestures from onlookers. She crossed her legs and turned sideways so that most of her thighs were exposed. Her pale white skin glistened. Tobias wondered what it would feel like to touch her skin. He cleared his throat and gulped half of the water. He sighed, glad that he didn't embarrass himself by choking.

She smiled and looked at him provocatively, leaning forward, so the low-cut V of her dress revealed a lot of her chest area. It beckoned him in a way he couldn't quite describe. He drained the rest of his water. The water wasn't doing him much good - he needed something stronger, then the waiter appeared with the menu. His relief was short-lived as he felt something brush his groin. He nearly jumped out of his skin.

It was only when it was time to place their orders that she realized that his jaws were slack, and his pupils dilated. He couldn't even look at her.

She looks stunning. Braces are gone. She's changed the way she wears her hair. The surgeon has given her a good nose.

The sleeveless V-neck dress she wore wasn't sitting well with the lower part of his body. He'd forgotten how much he enjoyed listening to Belinda. Unlike the monotonous ramblings of his wife, she always had something interesting to talk about. He remembered the first day they had met: he was in detention and was called out to meet his private tutor. She was studying to be a teacher and was working part-time as a private tutor.

Time flew by as they reminisced. The manager had to tap Tobias' shoulder to let them know the restaurant was closing for the day. Fortunately, his last meeting was just before lunch; he decided to walk her to her house so they could talk. He deftly avoided discussions concerning his wife each time Belinda tried to bring it up.

"Why don't you come in?" she asked and gestured.

No, no, no! Get out of here like right now! "I need something to soothe my headache," he said remorsefully.

"Sure, you do. Come in." Belinda beamed and waltzed into the house gesturing to his left and walked to the end of the corridor.

They drank some more wine, and she massaged his feet until he was lightheaded. He tried to get up but was a little drowsy. Frowning, he shook his head; he couldn't drive in this state and was better off ordering a taxi. He scanned the scantily clad room; it didn't look like she kept Yellow Pages around. The house was relatively simple, save the chandelier that matched the table lamps in the sitting room and the 72-inch TV.

Ten minutes later she handed him a glass of water and two caplets. He swallowed the pills, gulping the water noisily, and apologized. "Do you have the number of a taxi I can call?"

"Of course!" She bent down and deftly unbuckled his belt and undid his zip.

He reluctantly shoved her away. "Excuse me." *I have to leave. Any minute longer, I wouldn't be able to stop myself.* He tried to get up and plopped back on the sofa, holding his head. "Belinda, the taxi number. Please," he said, a little irritated.

"I never told you what I needed help with. I feel so silly now," she said and quickly sat on him, wiggling around.

Tobias got up and staggered, everything in his sight was hazy. As he looked down at her, his vision cleared. She was completely naked. He knew he had to leave and grimaced, but couldn't force his feelings to follow his head. His manhood, his head, and his heart each throbbed to a different frequency but the first seemed to be the only one he understood. The headache doubled. He sat back down, giving in.

As he massaged his forehead to soothe the headache, he wondered why his clothes were suddenly very soft and the sensation warm and strange. Belinda slowly climbed on top of him and swallowed him up in her warmth. He sighed, relaxed, and enjoyed the flow until his legs became numb. When it was over, he felt relief, anger and then guilt. He asked her where her bathroom was and went to it, but when he saw only female sanitary items, he walked out of the room. He tucked his shirt in and zipped up quickly, trying to think.

Overwhelmed with guilt, he picked up his jacket, which he didn't remember taking off. He didn't even remember taking off his shoes or his tie. He searched his pockets for his car keys. He had to leave now because his manhood had started to throb again. He half-limped to his car and reclined his chair.

He saw the time and winced. It was eleven p.m. He never stayed out late without informing his wife, and never this late. He had to think of the perfect excuse. He was already overcome by her incessant nagging and didn't wish for an increment in that department. He checked his phone and saw fifteen missed calls. He didn't need to see her name to know who the caller was. What he needed was a perfect excuse.

Tobias smiled.

He knew what to do.

He fastened his seatbelt and ignited the engine. He was about to drive off when he heard a screech of tyres. He apologized, but the person was too concerned with swearing at him to notice. Slowly, he pulled into Bridge Street and parked his car near the skaters' park. He looked surreptitiously around. Seeing no one, he walked across the park to the stream and drenched himself in it. He threw off his coat and rolled on the muddy bank, tore his shirt, then rushed back to his coat and removed the wads of twenty-pound notes and coins from his wallet and shoved them into his coat pocket. The wallet was dry, he noticed, so he went back to the water to soak it.

He pondered for a few minutes then took out the SIM and erased his information from the phone before tossing it to the other end of the park. He pinched himself, then walked into the bench, and the final touch was punching himself in the face.

He walked back to his car and drove home. When he got out of his car, he staggered and limped, shielding his face with his hands when he saw his neighbour. He increased his pace until she was inside her house. He continued the pretence until he got into his house.

When he got to his door, he inhaled a few times deeply before opening it. As he walked in, he didn't see his wife. She would have waited up for him so she could give him a piece of her mind. Assuming she was in bed, he walked to their room on tiptoes.

As soon as Jane set eyes on her husband, she knew something was different about him. Overwhelmed with the strange feeling that her greatest fear had been made manifest, she bit her lower lip and blinked back tears.

It was the first time she had indeed smelled a woman's perfume on him. It still filtered through the smell of algae and stale beer; the first time in their marriage that he didn't nuzzle and kiss her neck; the first time he didn't call out her name before he turned on the TV. He never brought it home. Even when they were almost bankrupt, he didn't bring it home. It wasn't work.

Jane inhaled deeply. She switched on the light and

pretended to be shocked on seeing him. She stretched out of the wheelchair, but Felicity was quick to force her back into it, then rushed out to get her crutches.

Jane waited for Felicity to leave and locked the door.

Picking up her cane, Jane waited a few minutes before joining her husband in the bathroom. She didn't probe him. She just nursed his wounds and was quiet the rest of the night. They were now even, and it would not happen again.

For the past five years that they've been together, Tobias had never known her to be this quiet. He couldn't sleep; he had a feeling that she had found out. Jane and Belinda didn't like each other. What if Belinda had told on him? He had not needed to walk Belinda home. He didn't even need to go into her house, headache, or no headache. He looked at his wife, wondering how he was going to explain himself.

Tobias wrinkled his nose when he felt the warm sun on his face. He pulled the pillow from under his head to shield his face. He'd promised to add blinds to the window. *I'd better add it to my 'to-do' list,* he thought then stiffened when he felt something between his thighs.

Enjoying the sensation, he didn't want it to stop. He winced when he felt a pinch on his manhood. A little startled, he threw the covers off, to see his wife's head bobbing up and down. Looking into her eyes as she took him in her mouth, he knew their relationship had turned blissful.

Black Eye

You are wondering what I'm doing here, with a black eye and bruises across my fair skin? I'll tell you right after I take these medications...

Well, here it goes.

My name is Kathleen Ibiwari Blue-Jack, a Kalabari girl, from the riverine part of Rivers State where the girls are born with naturally beautiful hair, lovely shaped legs, and glowing skin. It could be a curse sometimes because you yearned to be curvy like the upland girls or be like everyone else.

I finished my youth service three years ago today. It was hard to get a job because I refused to surrender my feminine gizmo.

My cardinal rule was and has been; 'never date a married man'. Most of the lecturers in my department were cavalier (or as I like to say, canter-and-lope) about girls and marital status didn't deter them. Because of this, I applied my mother's facial scrub on my face. I was terribly allergic to it. Seriously, my skin was always covered in rashes, and I didn't wear make-up. It was probably why I wasn't lucky enough to go on a date while at university.

Oh! My black eye, yes. It sort of started four months ago. I had to travel to Lagos for a job interview. The interview was a façade as they had already filled the position, the announcement was a formality. I got to the park to catch a bus to Port Harcourt a little too late and missed the last one. Hungry, I went to a *buka* to get myself dinner and was waylaid by hoodlums. They took everything - even my ticket.

Then it rained. For two hours the rain pelted me as if I had offended it. Tired, hungry and cold, I sat on a stone beside the unsheltered bus stop morbidly staring at passing cars. I was a stranger in this city, and I didn't even have a phone, embarrassing, I know.

Finally, the rain stopped. I got up just as a black jeep slowed down in front of me. I quickly stretched my hand to pick a big stone and held it behind me. The tinted windscreen was wound down and the light turned to reveal the driver. A man who looked rather young for the white hair on his head. I gasped and let go of the stone in my hand. It landed on my foot. I choked back my yelp and my eyes watered.

"Are you okay?" he asked, his brows arched.

I nodded.

His frown deepened. "Are you sure?"

"Go-good evening." I croaked and cleared my throat wondering for a second if that came out from me.

"I don't live here, but I do know it's not a safe place for anyone."

"I'm stranded," I said before I could stop myself, probably because he was the first person I had really spoken to since I left Port Harcourt.

"Get in," he beckoned and opened the door.

"I," I hesitated for a second, but the warm air that came out of the car felt so good. I hastily plopped onto the seat.

"Where were you heading to?" he asked, frowning.

"Port Harcourt." I wanted to tell him I had just got in, but I didn't think it was wise.

"Oh, where do I drop you then?"

I was surprised by the question that I didn't answer immediately.

"You're not from around here, are you?" he asked and nodded. "I'll drop you at the nearest hotel then."

He dropped me at a hotel. I lingered waiting for him to

leave so I could sneak out of there. It was when I saw him beside me that I realised he had made a U-turn. "I figured you might need money for your hotel bill, so here," he

produced wads of five hundred naira notes from his wallet and offered it to me. It was a wonder that my eyes remained in their sockets. If I had ever seen that amount of money at one go, then it was most certainly in a dream. Each note was brand new, even the smell of being untouched lingered. I thanked him then he asked, "Why were you here? I mean in Lagos."

I lowered my head. "I was here for an interview, but the spot has been taken."

He leant back on his seat. A car horn blared, irritating me immensely. He leant towards me and opened the door. "Get in."

179

I did and we drove away. A few minutes later, we parked on the roadside. My heart beat so rapidly that I held my breath for a few seconds, inhaled and exhaled deeply at intervals, to steady it.

"Your qualification?"

"I have a degree in Secretarial Administration from the University of Science and Technology in Port Harcourt. A two-one, diploma in computer appreciation -"

"Good, you can type. Would you like to work for me?"

"Mhm?" I was sitting beside a handsome guy who was no less than six feet tall. So, I was surprised by the question. Well, more than surprised... I think the word I'm looking for is thrilled. You know that there are times when you know something is wrong with your decision, but you go ahead with it? That was me at that moment. I must confess, he was quite distracting in a terribly good way.

He smiled, and I shivered.

"You need a job. My executive assistant resigned recently, and I'm yet to find a replacement. You could work for me, at least until you get a better job."

As I tried hard not to stare as he massaged the stubble of hair on his chin, I began to feel thirsty. I couldn't believe that tiny stalks of hair could look so good. I almost forgot that I had just seen a wedding band. It was quite conspicuous; it could irritate a person with photosensitive epilepsy, not a good example, but you catch my drift.

He was married. Of all the men in the world, a married man tickled my fancy and caused me to shiver in all the unholy places of my body. This was a disaster waiting to happen, so the best option would be to leave.

"I'll pay you a hundred and fifty thousand naira a month. You'll not need to come to work on the days I'm away. You may have to work at odd hours in an emergency, but I'll pay you overtime in those circumstances."

Everything else he said was lost because I was building a hundred-and-fifty-thousand-naira expenditure in my mind. I heard him clear his throat, but it was not until he tapped my shoulder that I realised I was still in his car.

"Mhm?"

"You are going to think about it, yes?"

"I'll take it," I replied a little loudly. It was too late to hide my desperation. I needed a job a. s. a. p. What with my mother's dialysis, my sister's WAEC fees coming up, and the house rent. I cleared my throat and added quietly. "When do I start?"

"Today?" he asked with a smile and explained. "I'm swarmed. You can work without supervision, yes?"

"Of course."

"Since, you're new in Lagos. I'll be your chauffeur for a week until I can attach you to someone from work. If we're lucky, you will get a place within the week. After two weeks, the hotel bills will rest on you should you continue to stay."

I nodded.

"Maybe you should rest today and start tomorrow," he murmured thoughtfully as he stared at the dashboard.

"Oh no o! I'm ready to start working right now."

"It's five o'clock in the morning," he retorted with a frown.

"I won't fall asleep, I assure you."

"Very well then," he sighed. "Are you sure?"

I nodded.

He drove me back to the hotel then talked to the receptionist. As I sat in the lounge watching them, *jealousy wan kill me*, but as a Port Harcourt girl, I maintained my cool. When he was done, he came over to me and handed me a key and a piece of paper.

"First floor, left wing," he said, pointing towards the lift. "I'll be back by nine."

I nodded and went to the lift.

A few days after I started working for him, I met the former executive assistant. She was a chubby, jovial, with a fully loaded frontline. Initially, I thought it could be the boss' child (you know the stories of bosses and their secretaries) until a man came into the office to pick her up and she introduced him as her husband. He doted on her so much that I was overwhelmed with envy. The only doting my boyfriend had ever shown me was to take me to an eatery for ice cream, which I ended up paying for.

The following week, while I was typing up a memo he needed for an advertising company, a woman barged in. She had an air of authority about her; her perfume filled the air, and her hair bounced. The blue linen dress she wore complimented her blue eyes. It was the first time I'd seen an ebony woman with blue eyes. I hoped she didn't see me scowl as I pretended not to notice her. I sneaked a look at the receptionist who was never at her desk downstairs, she was trying to look busy but ended up looking like someone scuttling aimlessly.

The lady looked at me then opened the door to my boss' office and slammed it shut without going in. I raised my head, looked at the door then at her and raised a brow. She smiled coolly at me and opened the door again. Before I could say anything, she slipped in, leaving it open. I went in after her. My boss looked up and discharged me. I nodded politely but was fuming. I knew she was of some importance to him. It wasn't until I heard raised voices that I knew there was more between them; she was his wife.

It was soon time for lunch; she had been in there for almost two hours. I knocked; no one answered. I knocked again, and she opened the door, appraised me with a grimace and brushed past me. I looked in to let him know I was leaving for lunch, but his head was in his hands, a habit I now knew was attributed to being overwhelmed.

I quietly withdrew. I was about to close the door when I heard my name and stopped to listen. I heard it again, my boss was calling me just as the love-struck Otobong Douglas a.k.a. Ajebó was calling me.

I smiled weakly at Ajebó, he nodded and gestured that I call him.

Fat chance!

He seemed too needy, and I wasn't ready to get grubby with him. He was as tall as my boss, fair, lanky but lithe. He got the attention of the girls in the business complex, but he had his eyes on me. I loved being the centre of a man's attention even though I wasn't interested in him plus I never got to pay for my lunch.

I went to meet my boss. He gestured to the chairs in which his guests sat. I pretended not to notice and remained standing. All I could think of was, take this opportunity as an advantage, so I took nervous strides towards him. When I got behind him, I took a deep breath, stretched out my hands and began to massage his neck; it was not until he leaned back sighing, that I realised I had been holding my breath.

Thirty minutes later, I heard voices outside his office, suspecting lunch break was over. I suspended what I was doing, picked up a set of files from the tray, and walked out of his office.

I set the files down and sighed. My sigh; a mild mixture of excitement and worry. Just as I was about to sit down, a rotund man called Chief Jeremy walked in unannounced. Not having an appointment, I asked him to wait. I didn't immediately confer with my boss. I just took my time dialling his office phone, we had two phones: one was for looking polite, and the other was for business. I figured that it was unfair to take out my frustration on the poor man, so I went into my boss' office.

I conferred with my boss like nothing had happened and he asked me to usher Chief Jeremy in. After their meeting, Chief Jeremy came and hovered around my desk. I ignored him; he was beginning to irritate me and I was tired of keeping a smiley face. After a while, he folded his arms and stood directly in front of me. I reciprocated by expressing my distaste.

"I see, you can't be bullied. So here," Chief Jeremy smiled timidly and shoved his hand into a wallet the size of a Bible. When he withdrew his hand, it was wrapped around a bundle which still had its bank tag. He tossed it at me, smiled, and nodded then leaned over my desk with a chuckle.

"*Omo too dun*, there is more where that came from," he murmured with a wide grin and raised his brow several times.

"Ibiwari," my boss called. Startled at the closeness of his voice I looked up. He had stuck his head out of his office.

"Sir," I said, quickly getting up.

"Ignore him." He turned to the man. "Don't you have something better to do?"

"When I see something this radiant?" Chief Jeremy gestured, chuckling even louder.

"Leave my staff alone." My boss said in a serious tone. From the corner of my eyes, I could see him leaning on the wall, his arms crossed, with a brow raised. He was so easy on the eye I had to bite the inside of my cheek to still my giddiness; my insides had now turned to melted wax.

I couldn't help noticing the cat-eyes my colleagues were giving him. I felt so proud when he didn't notice them. I may not be as beautiful as the other girls in the office, but no one needed eagle-eyes to peruse my *rack*.

My head was in the cloud. I had just finished all I had to type to stay in my woolgathering moment uninterrupted when I heard my name being mentioned. It was said so softly I assumed it was my gossiping colleagues. I couldn't resist fantasising about my boss, I was chewing my forefinger vehemently designing my fantasies that I didn't realise that it wasn't the cloud outside that was shielding the sun but my boss casting his shadow over me until he tapped on the table.

I abruptly got up, hitting my knees and croaked. "Sir!"

"Prepare a memo. The auditors will be here earlier than anticipated on the twenty-sixth of this month to be precise."

I frowned. *Two weeks early.*

Frowning, he asked. "Are you alright?"

"Ye-es sir!"

He thinned his lips and raised a brow and returned to his office.

The weeks that ensued my boss, the three accountants from Abuja, Ibrahim, Chika and Otobong, the financial secretary Tarun and her assistant Greg, Kadija from human resources, and I worked late into the night. Coincidentally, Isobel was out of the country for a retreat.

On one of such occasions, while we were taking a break, Ibrahim received a phone call and got up abruptly. "I'm going to be a father!" he exclaimed, shaking his fist in the air gleefully.

Everyone stared at him, some confused, others embarrassed and I was amused; we all knew his wife would soon put to bed.

Irritated, Tarun glowered at him. "You mean your wife has gone into labour, *abi?*"

Ibrahim nodded animatedly.

Tarun looked at him from head to toe and clucked her

tongue, "Mtcheew."

Ibrahim nodded animatedly again, still not getting what she was trying to tell him.

"And you're still here?" my boss asked, adjusting his tie.

We instantly became busy.

"Sir –"

"Go and be by your wife now!" my boss ordered and gestured at Tarun.

"Thank you, Sir. God bless you, Sir!" Ibrahim shrugged at Kadija, Chika and Greg. He usually gave them a lift home as they lived in the same area.

Kadija waved nonchalantly and mumbled. "We will find our way, don't worry."

"It's okay, go with him. The rest of us can hold the fort."

The relief in their hurried departure I would have envied if I hadn't been looking for a reason to eliminate these pawns of hindrance. A few hours later, sleep clawed at my eyelids, but I needed to keep a watchful eye for an opening. Otobong stretched, and I yawned simultaneously. He smiled and winked at me when he noticed.

Otobong stretching again and murmured, "Boss, I'll be off to my office for a nap if you don't mind?"

My boss waved at him offhandedly.

Otobong got up and tucked his feet in his shoes then tilted his head at me to join him.

Fat chance!

I spread my hands over the papers that lay on my laps. I was long done with them but couldn't let anyone know, could I? Tarun scuttled after him. I waited for about thirty minutes and decided to *use* the toilet. I didn't need to reach it to hear Otobong snoring. I heard the main door open and tiptoed towards it to see Tarun kiss a man who was too fair, too muscular and too tall to be her husband.

I giggled.

186

She was always prim and proper and spoke against cheating wives like she was born to do just that. I took off my shoes, and my bladder decided to show itself strong. I thought it was just nerves, but the pressure below my stomach was building, and I rushed to the toilet. I cleaned myself and ran to my boss' office pausing at the door to catch my breath by huffing and puffing quickly. When I walked in his hands were on his face, a bottle with tea-coloured liquid which I later discovered was whisky stood on the floor close to his feet. He looked up at me rubbing his chin.

"Want some?"

I nodded.

He opened a cabinet by his feet, produced another glass, and poured some for me.

I nodded my thanks and took a sip then squeezed my eyes shut and tightened my grip around the glass and the edge of the table as my throat burned. I cleared my throat and opened my eyes.

He was looking at me, amused. Again, my throat went dry. I quickly gulped the remainder, which wasn't a good idea.

"You took it well," he said with a chuckle. "My wife, she didn't..." he continued talking; he lost me at 'my wife'. I had to plaster a smile on my lips to look interested and absentmindedly kept topping up his drink, he kept drinking. I stopped as soon as I realised what I was doing, but he was already tipsy. I watched him lean back on his chair.

I thanked the heavens for the opportunity. He had been chewing groundnut, so he wasn't out of his wits. But watching him lean back on his recliner languorously was doing unimaginable things to my body, I swear. As I stared at him the little courage I had filtered away like water through a sieve, my heart palpitating, my legs weak and wobbly and my hands shaking. I longed for him more than words could say. I tried to keep my shaking, sweaty hands steady and my elbows brushed the bottle, and I remembered. If I took a sip and tried to seduce him and fail? I could blame it on the alcohol.

He would too. He'd had more than I did.

I gulped the whole glass. My head expanded as I shuddered from head to toe. I took a step forward and paused. Then I bit my cheek as I took another step until I was standing in front of him, right between his legs then I froze. Seconds passed into minutes, but I couldn't move. I couldn't even fidget. Then he stirred and turned his head which lolled back into its former position.

Suddenly, I was overcome with the most primal urge to touch his face. By this time, my breathing was ragged. I stretched one shaky hand to his face and bit my forefinger in the other for support. As soon as I touched his face and he nuzzled my hand, everything else fell apart. I opened the button of his shirt as I gingerly leaned in to kiss him. There was no resistance. He kissed me back.

For months, I had thought of this moment. Now, I didn't want to hold back. I forgot how I wanted to slowly ravish him until all his waking moments were filled with thoughts of me. I had worn a wraparound outfit almost every day for the past three months, pining for this moment. Now there was no need to be modest. So, I loosened the string that bound the dress to my waistline.

An hour later, we left the office together. He spent the weekend at my house, where I showed off my culinary skills. I didn't mind that he had to leave Sunday evening to pick up his wife.

Slow and steady to win the race, I told myself.

188

On Monday, he held back. He was back to his old self, so I assumed it was because we were in a working environment and he wanted to focus on the auditors who always seemed to be at the *right* place and at the *right* time. For three weeks, the auditors hovered. While the auditors were still around, the company won an award. My boss was so pleased he decided to throw a huge party that weekend.

I wore a white wraparound dress because white was his favourite colour – don't ask me how I found out. I wore just a little makeup so smudges could easily be tidied up. I was amongst the team that would tidy up so I was ready to give him another nice time since his wife would be in Abuja for the weekend.

The party was in full swing. I held the champagne flute as I'd seen in the movies, sipped from it and almost choked. I was nervous, and for the first time in my life, I really felt alone. I didn't know anyone in the office well enough to be friends with them; they seemed to chaperon the wolf-pack thing. To distract me from myself, I drank more champagne and wove more dreams of what I'd do to win my boss over to my side.

Somehow, Isobel materialised in the dream I wove. I gritted my teeth and tried to keep her out. It took me a while to notice that it was the real Isobel in front of me with a cool smile in her haughty demeanour, the Isobel that was supposed to be in Abuja. She wore a dress similar to mine, but hers was more daring. She walked towards me. I turned away and took another glass of champagne and gulped it down. Tarun nodded at me as she walked past Isobel and I replied with a small smile.

189

I turned my attention to the people dancing in the middle of the room. Not long after I felt someone tap me on the shoulder. I turned right into a closed fist. It felt like

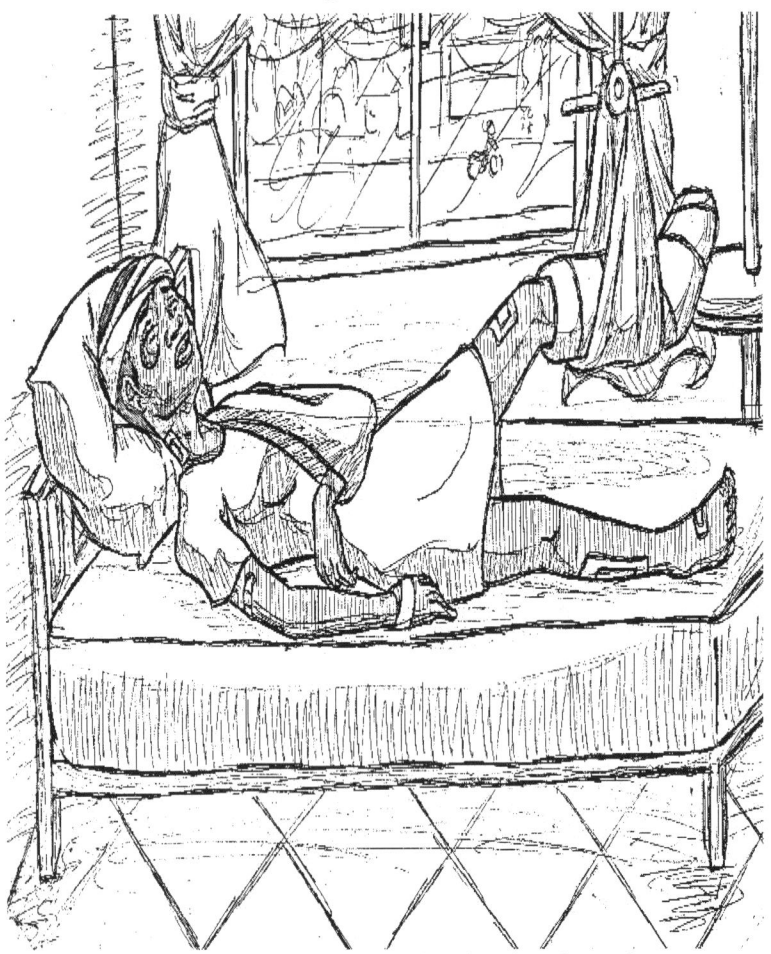

something was jiggling in my head right after that. I lost my balance and the next thing I knew I was on the ground with champagne glasses around me, I was wet, my skin pinched, but I couldn't scratch it. My ears were ringing. My vision was playing tricks on me as everything went in and out of focus, and I didn't know where I was. I could only remember reprimanding myself for wearing those ridiculous heels.

I remember trying to wiggle out of Otobong's tight grip. I shuddered when I heard the siren. I thought she had called the police on me.

Don't blame me! I didn't know how things worked in Lagos. Besides, her twin brother was the commissioner of police.

I do remember Isobel saying something and laughing. I couldn't make out the words then, but now I do: *Frederick told me everything.*

I later found out that Tarun had taken a few pictures of me – I was wearing nothing underneath the lower part of my dress. She had a video that showed Otobong putting pressure on my calf where I had a major laceration. I had taken down half of the champagne tower.

So, you see, that is what happened. The disadvantage of being so fair-skinned is that no amount of foundation can conceal a black eye.

Boomerang

"You're not my real mum, anyway," Samantha said in a high-pitched voice.

"I care about you," the new Mrs Gordon said.

"You just want to take my dad from me."

Mrs Gordon raised her hands in frustrated surrender.

Samantha stormed out of the kitchen. She was having a hard enough time at school and didn't need some broad her father brought in to bother her. As she sat on her bed, she grumbled and only stopped when her phone began to ring. Seeing her best friend Tilly's face on the screen, she grumbled the more. She'd missed out on a lot of outings with Tilly because of Andy. If only she had taken Tilly's advice and stayed away from Andy's kind, *the popular bad boy,* she wouldn't be in this predicament.

She reached out for the pregnancy test strips on the bureau and perused them yet again, willing the lines to change. She grimaced, and her shoulders sunk. Andy was gentle, handsome, and knew the right things to say and at the right time, too. She had even believed him when he told her that Tilly was just bitter because he didn't reciprocate her advances towards him.

She wiped the tears off from her face and sank to the ground as the bed no longer felt comfortable. On hearing footsteps, she dashed to the door and slid the bolt. Her eyes fell on her mother's picture on her desk, and more tears dripped from her eyes.

She had promised her mother that she would wait until she was twenty-one before venturing into an intimate relationship. But then, her mother had promised her that she would always be there for her. Even her father had promised that nothing would come between them. It was barely a year ago that they buried her mother and her dad brought in a woman who could be mistaken for her mother except for the auburn head of hair. Andy had promised. Tilly had promised. Grandma had promised. Even her step-grandpa had promised. All any one of them had done was promise. But none, no, not one kept their promises.

Her phone was beeping. She looked at the LCD and snickered. Ignoring it on the nightstand she walked to her desk, turned up the music, and plopped back on her bed.

How could she have known Andy was a douchebag? They had attended the same playgroup and kindergarten. He used to sneak into her garden when the fence was broken, and they'd play in her pink rickety treehouse for hours. There was a time she pretended to be sick, and her mother left her at home, and he snuck out of his house to see her while his babysitter remained rooted on the sofa facing the TV shooting up his parents' itemised account for phone bills.

They even shared the same dentist.

She had always had a huge crush on him from the day she could talk. Why did she not come home that night? She wasn't even supposed to be at that party in the first place. It was the first time she had ever gate-crashed. How could she have known that she would be on everyone's mobile phone after just one unplanned night with her dream boyfriend? Now, she had no friends and no lover, and her father has been stolen from her by a woman who wants to take her mother's place, the butt of everyone's joke. She hated her life now.

She bit her nails vigorously; maybe there was something she could do. She couldn't get back at Arringdale Tucker High School, but she was definitely going to get back at Andy.

The new Mrs Gordon winced as she heard the slamming of the door. She heard another slam and twirled around to see a man grinning at her. She smiled back until she looked down and saw muddy shoes and water dripping on the mat.

"Hello, dearie!" Doctor Gordon cheerfully murmured.

"Hey, mister!" The new Mrs Gordon murmured, her arms akimbo, tapping one foot.

His forehead furrowed.

She pointed at his feet.

He smiled and took off his shoes and his mac, opened the door leading to the patio, dropped them, and closed the door. He arched his brows, and she replied with a shrug, smiling then he walked to her and planted a kiss on her forehead. Overwhelmed with several emotions to care about his wet clothes anymore, she shivered in his embrace. She wiped her tears just before he pulled her away gently to study her face.

194

"What's going on?" he asked, frowning.

She smiled ruefully, cupped his face as she looked into his eyes and whispered, "It's because I love you!" then planted a kiss on his lips before leaving the kitchen. There was a knock on the door, but she simply walked past it.

He went to answer it.

Six months ago

A week before last term's midterm break, after Buffalos, their basketball team had defeated the Eagles of Paddington High he took note of her. He didn't belong to the team, and he was almost certainly there for the cheerleaders.

The following day, as they were heading to class, he pulled her back and tucked a piece of paper in her hand. She was so curious that she opened it to see that he had scribbled his mobile number on it.

Ariana had been watching them. In a few seconds, she was beside Samantha and yanked the paper out of Samantha's hand, tossed it into her mouth, chewed and spat it into the bin before waltzing out of the class. Samantha was good with numbers and had already repeated it in her head several times before Ariana took the paper.

The following day, Samantha joined the cheer squad to spite Ariana, who was its captain. So, when they had an impromptu practice, she was the only one who didn't complain. After practice, Ariana tugged her away to a corner of the sports hall.

"Sammie, I like you a whole lot, that's why you're still on this team. But if you continue to flirt with my boyfriend, I'll make life so miserable for -."

Samantha did a mock shudder, sniggered, and sauntered away. The rest of the team stared at one girl, then the other in confusion. Ariana turned her back to everyone while she tried to steady her breath, digging her nails into her palms at the same time.

As they emptied their lockers, Tilly asked Samantha, "What was that about?"

"Andy," Samantha drawled.

Tilly, wearing a confused face, asked, "Who's Andy?"

Samantha was waving and smiling sheepishly at someone. Tilly turned to see who it was. "Oh! That Andy," she muttered, rolling her eyes.

The following day Samantha slipped a note into Andy's locker. The preceding weeks he and she were seen a couple of times at his father's lodge after school hours – he took Samantha there because that was the only place Ariana didn't know about. Whenever his father was at the lodge, Samantha brought him home.

Two months later, while they were at his father's lodge, he left her a note and snuck out. She got dressed in the fancy dress he had bought her and went to meet him at the party. That was the day she became the school's porn sensation. He had made an internet diary of them sexting which culminated in the deed that had her in her present predicament.

Ironically, his face wasn't anywhere in the diary.

Last Month

The school's football team had had a friendly match with a neighbouring school, and the boys were now in their locker room when Samantha waltzed in. She was wearing a red, promiscuously low-cut blouse for someone with large breasts like herself. Her navy-blue skirt precariously hitched up for a licentious audience and her newly shampooed hair was piled on the top of her head in a bun except for some carefree tendrils. She rouged her cheekbone to match her glossy lips.

The boys whistled, clapped, and hooted while closing in

to form a circle around her. She slanted her head, rubbed the nape of her neck slowly then started playing with a few tendrils of hair. As soon as Andy came out of one of the showers, she sauntered towards him. He reluctantly followed her towards the door to the first shower cubicle. The boys started howling when she tore the towel off from his waist.

She plastered kisses on his face and worked her way down towards his midriff. She paused, smiling mischievously, and continued descending. As soon as he was fully erect, she put her hand into her blouse and produced a little brown tube then squeezed its content - her special brand of hot sauce, stinging nettle, and poison ivy - on his manhood and whisked out of there.

He didn't react immediately. He stood completely still, turning red and breathing heavily then began to move like someone carrying something heavy between his legs as he rushed into the shower. Some of the boys followed his movement while others either jeered or patted his back.

She leaned on the door once she was outside the room and composed herself, glaring at anyone who stared at her or gave her a second look. Satisfied, she went to her locker, took out her backpack, and left the school premises.

She danced around the kitchen, singing as she brought out ingredients for a sandwich. Admiring her achievement, she took a bite and suddenly felt the urge to puke. Throwing the sandwich in the bin, she settled for pineapple juice. Carrying the glass of juice in one hand and a thriller novel in the other, she walked into the sitting room. It was only until she had slumped on the chair that she realised her stepmother was there.

Mrs Gordon had her legs and arms crossed as she stared blankly at Samantha.

Feeling uncomfortable, Samantha tried to shrug it off. Failing, she got up to leave.

"Not so fast," Mrs Gordon said in a steely voice.

Samantha would have ignored her, but for the tone of voice. "What do you want?"

"To know how far along you are."

"What?" Samantha asked, taken aback.

"You heard me, Samantha."

"Are you okay?" Samantha asked frowning.

"Probably. The question is, are you?"

Samantha's forehead furrowed deeper, and she turned to make her exit.

"How old is your pregnancy?"

Samantha felt like she had just swallowed a bitter pill and was simultaneously dunked in ice water.

"What do you intend to do about it? Tell my dad?" she dared her stepmother. Feeling smothered, she found that her legs could no longer carry her and sat back in the chair, holding her head as she moaned.

"I'll not tell your father because I believe you should do it yourself, as soon as you can, that is."

Samantha gave her an ugly look.

"And that is if you want to keep it."

"I don't."

Mrs Gordon raised a brow and pursed her lips.

"I want an abortion. I need to finish school."

"Samantha, I am -," Mrs Gordon started to say in staccato.

"Oh no, no, no, I can't have a baby! I'm too young for this!" Samantha uttered in a hushed tone.

"Samantha, I..."

"Please help me. You're my mom, after all." Samantha murmured indignantly.

"Interesting concept. Mom. I'm afraid you're on your own in this."

"So much for being *my mom*." Samantha scoffed. "Thanks for nothing!"

"You're welcome. You will, however, have to put up with me. And I, you, because your dad will be away for about six months. It was impromptu -"

Samantha glared, scoffed again and stalked out of the room. She avoided Mrs Gordon like the plague until Mrs Gordon had to take her to the hospital for alcohol poisoning. A few hours later, she was discharged, and the following week Mrs Gordon had to take her in again because she was bleeding – Samantha had tried a recipe she found online for terminating pregnancies.

After that, she took Samantha to all her antenatal appointments and monitored all her activities like a hawk eager to spring on its prey. Samantha refused to go with her to baby shops, so she gave her a voucher to shop online. Talking to Samantha was tedious, even though she knew the poor girl needed someone to talk to, so Mrs Gordon decided to surprise her stepdaughter by stripping the spare room and turning it into a nursery.

When all else failed, Samantha decided to starve herself to death. In the afternoon of the same day, what felt like a thousand needles stabbing her head caused her to change her mind. Anytime Mrs Gordon made up her mind to stop being Samantha's prop, her sympathetic side repealed that decision. For another two weeks, she didn't set eyes on Samantha; she'd prepare breakfast and set the tray down at Samantha's door before leaving for work. By the time she got back, the tray would be empty and clean. In the evening she'd do the same thing.

One evening she came back early and saw Samantha by the sink and her heart went to her. She looked bigger, and her face was much fuller and covered in acne. She walked on tiptoes so her heels wouldn't clack on the concrete floor and gently opened the door. Samantha heard the jingle of keys and turned around to make a quick exit. Mrs Gordon was already inside.

Unsuccessful at crossing her arms over her chest, she let them lay limply on her stomach and averted her gaze.

Mrs Gordon gestured. "Sit down."

Samantha walked to the sitting room and lowered herself gently into the sofa closest to her and looked at Mrs Gordon with watery eyes and mumbled, "thank you."

Two Days ago
Samantha massaged the side of her stomach that was throbbing. It was a very hot September day with no wind to counter the heat, the sweat dried as quickly as it came. As they sat on the porch, Samantha wondered how her stepmother was able to sleep through the heat.

She arched her back using her hand for support as she

tried to get up from the rocking chair and cursing herself for sitting in it in the first place. She sighed with relief when she finally got out of it then looked down at her stepmother with contempt, shook her head, and headed for the kitchen in search of something cold to drink.

Dr Gordon stood over his wife a few seconds after his daughter; Samantha had entered the house. He heaved his brown travelling bag from his shoulder and placed his laptop bag on top of it. He smiled at his wife's bemused smile and cleared his throat.

She was still sleeping.

He brushed her tousled hair off her face and rubbed her cheeks lovingly. "Hello, Dearie! Dreaming of me, I hope," he said when she opened her eyes.

"How long have I been out?" She asked groggily.

"I don't know. I came in round the back."

"I'm sorry, welcome," he said grinning lazily as she seductively winked at him. "I missed you!"

"I missed you, too," he said as they locked in an embrace.

"How was Yorkshire?" she asked curiously.

"I've got a lot to tell you. I need a cold drink first," he said, untangling himself. "Would you like anything?"

"Yes, I guess," she retorted, still groggy.

He cocked his head, arching his brow.

"I'll have what you're having," she said giggling. She had a feeling she was forgetting something but shrugged it off. He was supposed to be back in November. Then she slapped her forehead, remembering Samantha. Her husband wasn't yet aware of his daughter's pregnancy.

Dr Gordon looked curiously at the young woman who was sipping a glass of orange juice and rapidly flipping through a magazine on the counter. "Sammie?" he whispered, afraid that she was the one he was staring at, with a protruding stomach.

Samantha spun just as the drinking glass slipped from her hand. Slowly backing out of the kitchen, she stepped on the shards of glass and froze.

Dr Gordon, overwhelmed with concern, went to his daughter. While he carried his daughter, who was now red-faced and bleeding, into the living room. Mrs Gordon scampered into the kitchen to inform her husband of the new development, saw blood, and went to fetch the first aid kit.

The house was deafeningly quiet.

While Dr Gordon frettingly marched from one end of the room to the other, Mrs Gordon darted glances at her husband and stepdaughter who was now curled up in a corner.

Dr Gordon stopped abruptly, inclining his ear and continued to pace again then asked. "Who did you say is the father?"

Samantha curled up even further.

"Who's the father?" he asked again, this time his voice much colder and louder than before.

In response, Samantha started squalling.

Dr Gordon shook his head and walked out of the house.

It was seven o'clock the following day when the women who had fallen asleep in the sitting room were woken by the doorbell. Mrs Gordon ushered Samantha to get up after glancing through the muslin-like curtain and waited for Samantha to get to the landing. At the door, she paused, took a deep breath, and opened it. She frowned when she saw a plump middle-aged woman in dark green khakis at the door with her husband.

She opened the door wider to let them in. He was walking morosely behind the paramedic and staggered slightly when they got to the sitting room. The paramedic left almost immediately. He sat on a chair. Feeling uncomfortable, he slid to the floor. Mrs Gordon came and sat down beside him and took his hand in hers.

"What do I do?" he whispered as he laid his head on her shoulder.

"I don't know. She will be due in less than two months," she said, trying to conceal her worry while patting his hand.

Samantha had come down; she stood in the way of the sun's rays and was shivering and fidgeting.

"Daddy, I'm sorry! I really am."

"Who is the father?" he asked, his voice was low, a mixture of pain, sorrow, and sympathy.

"Excuse me!" Mrs Gordon said, getting up.

Her husband caught her arm in time. "You are staying. She is now your daughter," he muttered and turned to Samantha. "She's now your mother, the best you can get." He exhaled deeply, pleading with his eyes. "Sarah, we could use some advice."

The women were stunned.

"Well go on, ask her," he ushered his wife.

Mrs Gordon looked confused. "Ask her what?"

"No one is taking my mother's place." Samantha snapped, cautiously keeping her distance.

"Don't take that tone with me, young lady." He snarled and added with a softer tone. "No one is replacing your mother..." he paused, shaking his head. "I don't know what to do with you right now. I try my best to be a good father, and this is the thanks I get, yeah?"

The doorbell chimed right after Samantha hurriedly left the living room.

Dr Gordon raised a brow. "Are you expecting anyone?"

Mrs Gordon shook her head but went to answer the door. A thin woman cast a shadow across her. She had to look up at the five-foot-eight woman to see her face. The woman wore a thin smile, but her dimples still showed. She held her glossy, burnt orange hair off her face and squinted at the same time. Her slender legs were tucked in leather boots even though it was not yet spring. Her floral print dress stuck to her body, revealing more than a woman should see, much less a man. The woman cleared her throat as if meaning to get attention.

"Do I... sorry. How may I help you?"

"I need to speak to Ashley Gordon."

"Is it important? Because this is not a good time."

"That's not a problem. Just tell him it's Mrs Anubhuti Hendricks. Or better still..." the woman said as she forced her way in, dragging a teenager behind her.

"Who is it?" Dr Gordon asked as soon as his wife appeared.

Mrs Gordon shrugged. The woman trudged closely behind, still tugging the teenager.

"You don't remember me?" Anubhuti let out a throaty laugh. "Well, I don't have the time to start explaining as I have a flight to catch in..." she looked at her wrist and added, "less than an hour. This is Andy. I'm handing him over to you because he is, after all, your son."

"What?" Dr Gordon spat.

Mrs Gordon stared at the woman with an open mouth.

Andy froze.

"I'm sorry, but this is it. I have to move on, you know." She gestured and then turned to face Andy, patted his cheek and murmured. "If you need me, I'm a phone call away. I love you." She wrapped her arms around him, gave him a perfunctory kiss, and was about to leave when Mrs Gordon blocked her path.

"You're going nowhere until I know what's going on."

Mrs Hendricks sized Mrs Gordon up. "You don't want to know."

"Try me," Mrs Gordon said pointedly.

Mrs Hendricks let out a ragged sound. "Eighteen years ago, you," she cleared her throat and turned to face Mrs Gordon. "Your man here, drugged and raped me and said I'd given him consent. *This* is the product of *that* consent."

Samantha came back into the sitting room after easing herself and glared angrily at Andy, "What are you doing here? What do you want this time?"

Andy was still dazed. He looked down at her stomach and raised a brow.

Samantha wore a wicked grin and hissed. "It's *yours*."

"Oh my God!" Mrs Gordon exclaimed and fainted.

Andy ran out.

Samantha frowned, thinking it was the heat that caused her stepmother to pass out she limped-ran-walked to the kitchen to get water. When the cold water didn't wake her stepmother, she plopped onto the chair closest to the phone and dialled the hospital.

Dr Gordon hadn't noticed his wife pass out nor had he heard the conversation between his daughter and his son because he had buried his head between his thighs. Tears ran down his face as he reminisced the event from all those years ago. He desired to be part of the in-crowd. They'd given him the opportunity: it was the first time he'd had alcohol, had sex, been with a girl who'd shown interest. Consent? She didn't say no, did she? He was drunk himself and didn't mind that she was too. All he could hear was their cheering him on as he made out with her on the beanbag in the middle of the lounge. He should have known when he didn't see her again. But how was he supposed to have known? He didn't even know her name then.

Ego was a vice. An oyster of circles out to get you.

Acknowledgement

I would like to express my gratitude to everyone who has contributed to the writing of this book, directly and indirectly.

I would especially like to thank my mum who made me realise that there is beauty in every journey.

I would especially like to thank my optimistic children who taught me that a treasure chest can be as conspicuous as it is precarious.

GLOSSARIES

Akanchi – *Awele's scale of justice.*

Anya'ogu – *A special gift of sight that the Chieftain uses to locate an Okoruchi.*

Babeling – *A child under two.*

Bath-hut - *Bathroom.*

Birther - *Midwife.*

Chest piece – *a specially thinned animal skin used to cover the breast.*

Chieftain – *The bearer and caretaker of the Ófòr-Oguneli.*

Childling – *A child between two and eleven years old.*

Cycle (of seasons) - *A year.*

Damping-illusion – *A cloaking spell.*

De'nnâ – *A male parent.*

Divination – *Foretelling, prophecy.*

Dibia – *Soothsayer.*

Dugout - *Bunker.*

Ehuehus – *A person without supernatural gifts.*

Eli'ndiosunanjó - *A prison for the souls of the wicked, corrupt or evil.*

Enwere – *A sect of wood nymphs tasked with protecting the realm between realms.*

Flinchete – *Machetes made from flint.*

Flintsmiths – *Makers of flinchetes.*

Food hut – *A room for storing and cooking meals.*

Glamour – *Illusion.*

God-touch – *A blessing and a protection by the gods.*

Gourd-lanthorn – *lantern made from bottle gourd, tin, water and moss.*

Hamlet – *A settlement.*

Herald – *An aura.*

Hierarchies – *The pecking order of the Okoruchi.*

Imanwoke – *The third rite of passage of into manhood. A festival in which young men show off their mental prowess.*

Imaonyemgbu – *The second rite of passage of into*

manhood. *A festival in which young men show off their strength and skills.*

Insight – *Ability to sense things intuitively.*

Ité-mini – *Earthernware pot used for storing water.*

Lewd-hut – *A hut where women and men who engage in sexual intercourse for money are available.*

Life-force – *The essence of a person, blood.*

Merfolk – *Man, Men.*

Mermate – *The male spouse.*

Mini-Echichem – *A river in Rimeóku that souls cross and lose their thoughts in the process.*

Natal day – *The day of one's birth.*

Nimbus veils of mist/ nimbus(es) – *The essence of a herald.*

Nné – *A woman with a child or children.*

Nnénnya – *A female sibling.*

Nnéruka – *A male sibling.*

Nwô'm – *A name an adult calls a young stranger.*

Nwónna – *Offspring of the same father, uncle, etc.*

Nwónne – *Offspring of the same mother, aunt, etc.*

Nwónnenanna – *Offspring of the same parents, aunt, uncle, cousin.*

Nwónnénné - *Children of the same grandmother.*

Offshoot of offspring – *Grandson or granddaughter.*

Offspring (boy/girl) – *Son or daughter.*

Ófòr-Nkigwe – *King's scepter.*

Ófòr-Oguneli – *Chieftain's scepter.*

Okoruchis - *A living folks gifted with supernatural powers.*

Omeneri bottle – *A decanter used as a trap.*

Paramount Ruler - *An Okuruchi who was the most gifted in his talents.*

Pearls of Oko River - *Cloud-coloured stones found in the great Oko River. It turns red when magic was near and also deters its power.*

Quarter-of-a-moon – *Three hours, day or night.*

Sheathpoc– *Two-sided sheath for little valuables.*

Spirit-guide – *A supernatural guardian.*

Sprit– *A living folk's aura.*

Tanning moon tree - *A two-tone tree that glistened in the night, tea made with its bark induced a sleeping curse. It was rumoured to keep its victim asleep for a hundred cycles. It exists only in the realm of the Imperials.*

Totem cape – *A hide imbued with powers.*

Weefolk – *Woman, women or girl.*

Weemate – *A female spouse.*

Work hands – *A labourer.*

Youngling – *A child between twelve and twenty years.*

Yoyoma – *An older woman who seeks companionship in a younger man, usually sexual.*

Also, by Agnes Kay-E
Tainted Hearts – Women Fiction

Nicholas' First Nativity – Children's Fiction

The Girl From Home – Women Fiction

Also, as Kemka Ezinwo
Captured Within

Something New

Sneak Preview: Captured Within

1

The crispy august wind smacked Matthew Udoh. He could barely see through the fog, let alone, find the aluminium bucket. He hated the harmattan season because his skin would shrivel like the smoked mackerel his mother bought for dinner and then itch for hours. Should he open his mouth, his already chapped lips would tear; the last time it took weeks to heal. The sun wasn't out. He trembled at the thought of pouring cold water over his body. He shuddered: the escaping moon cast its reflection on the surface of the water in the bucket, reminding him of its icy coldness. Lifting a bowl full of water, he held his breath and threw the water over himself. The water landed on the ground with a light thud, splinters of it touching his feet – he had shifted before the water fell. His mother's voice echoed, rekindling the courage he needed.

I need oil on my skin, he thought. Then he winced touching his cheeks as the memory of when Eka-Effiòng's hand stroke his cheek resurfaced – he heard chirping much like the little blue birds that circled 'Tom's head in the *Tom and Jerry* cartoon which he and his friends had watched through a crack in the door of Ette Okon's house. He never understood how such a frail-looking woman could lash out such pain.

"I'll never take what doesn't belong to me again!" He

muttered to himself.

Thinking of *Tom and Jerry*, he smiled. Ette Okon would never have discovered how rats started getting into his house if Livinus had not gone bragging to his sisters.

His skin had started to itch, but he couldn't get his hands through his clothes because they were snug.

"Matthew!" his mother shouted from the back of the house. He could tell she was coming out of the bathroom from the sound of the zinc door.

"Have you eaten your food?" She asked in *Ibibio*.

She always brought a smile to his face probably because she was the only family he had or because she was easy to talk to. He was once told that his mum was the belle of the village, that she stood tall among her peers – still did, with long, black and glossy hair, that the superstitious suspected she was a *'mammy water'*. She was slender, and her dark skin glowed, her eyes shaped like cat's eyes stamped with hazel-coloured pupils. She had a small pointed nose, and her lips were small, all neatly tucked in an oval-shaped face. Nobody understood what she saw in his father - One minute he was in a good mood and then another he was in a bad mood. (No one knew about bipolar disorder then). Matthew was told he had his mother's looks, though he didn't see how.

His skin started itching again.

He rushed to where his food was and his eyes lit with joy. It was *garri* and palm kernel. His jaws hurt as he chewed, but he didn't care. It was like eating rice and chicken on Christmas day. He hurriedly ate his food as he didn't want his friends to see him soaking *garri*. Nevertheless, he couldn't help waiting for the *garri* to swell.

Matthew's mother, Matty, she was so called because it was shorter than calling her Eka-Matty, watched her son eat with relish and smiled and murmured, "Thank you, Jesus!" For weeks, they've been eating cooked unripe pawpaw. She knew he ate it to please her. He didn't beg, which often surprised her. She turned towards the door she was leaning on to hide her tears and pray. *Please, God. Look not on my sins. Look on the faith I have in you and take my son away from this misery. Please don't let him grow up in poverty.*

"Mummy, I have finished eating o," Matthew said and wiped his mouth.

Smiling, she wiped away her tears.

"Mmami, thank you."

"You're welcome, dear child. I have a surprise for you."

Eka-Matty undid one end of her wrapper, loosening the tip to reveal scrunched-up money. She gave it to him. She opened the door to withdraw something in a black cellophane bag: it was a pair of slippers. The money was from the sale of palm kernel: it wasn't enough to cover both his school fees, and a pair of sandals. Matthew jumped up and down in excitement, and then wiggled his waist and jumped on his mother who started laughing. He was glad to be paying his fees on the first day of school; something that had never happened before.

His friends, Livinus Orhiunu and Ambrose Livingstone arrived just as he was putting the money into his pocket. Livinus was talkative and chubby in an intimidating way; even the senior prefects feared to flog him whenever he was late. His father even suspected him of stealing food at night. His father never caught him because he did it in the afternoon.

Ambrose, on the other hand, was lanky, reserved and taller than most people his age with four older brothers of which, three were now late, and seven sisters. His mother and Matthew's mother got along but weren't friends, which was expected as Ambrose's mother was old enough to be Matthew's mother.

They arrived at school late because Livinus had forgotten something, again. Mr Kalabór, the duty Master, was at the entrance of the school with his *koboko*. The staff and students of Saint Barnabas Primary School, Kono didn't take kindly to this his *koboko*. No one openly objected because Mr Kalabór was related to the Headmaster. However, some teachers shielded their children and played the 'mind-your-business' game when it came to the other students.

Mr Kalabór glared sternly at them. "Why are you always late? I let you pass yesterday, but that is not happening today. Kneel!"

Matthew was already shaking like a leaf under heavy rain. He gave everyone six strokes of his *koboko,* but when it got to Matthew's turn, he frowned, maybe because he was afraid the boy would die. He quickly thought of a way to protect his reputation.

Mr Kalabór hissed at Matthew. "Come with me!"

Matthew followed.

When they got to the staffroom, his frown was replaced with concern.

"Sit down. Are you all right?" Mr Kalabór asked softly.

Matthew's reply was inaudible. His eyes glazed, his mouth watered as the different aromas of displayed food hit him. A staff on maternity leave had sent food from the celebration of the safe delivery of her first son. Mr Kalabór noticed how the little boy's eyes danced from one dish to another, offered to get him some food but Matthew refused. Mr Kalabór got a paper plate and filled it up with food.

"I won't tell if you won't." Mr Kalabór whispered.

Before Mr Kalabór could say, 'A', Matthew was slurping and gulping away with such speed that the star-nosed mole would envy, and a grass cutter would relish. He had just finished eating and was wiping his mouth with the back of his hand when a light-skinned girl walked in, pulled by the ear into the room by Miss Boyd. Her skin shone like Ette Okon's Sunday shoes after it had been waxed with the Kiwi polish he claimed was a souvenir. She was so thin it looked like a feather could knock her down, with her nose as pointy as the cones they were told to make in class last term, and her hair was brown and curly. Matthew stared at her. He only realized his mouth had been open when he accidentally swallowed something: *saliva, a fly?*

She giggled covering her mouth to muffle the sound.

He looked over at Miss Boyd whose hand was still on the girl's ear. The girl looked a lot like her even though Miss Boyd's face was covered in pimples. *She must be the new girl that Livinus' sisters were talking about yesterday; I can almost swear they were jealous.* He remembered he had seen her with Mfon when he went with his mother to sell palm kernel.

The Labour Master came in, saw Matthew and grunted, "Don't you have a class you should be in?"

Before the teacher could utter another word, Matthew ran as fast as his wobbling legs could carry him. He couldn't understand why his legs were suddenly wobbly.

From where she was standing she could see him run to his class. It was her class too. *Very white teeth for a village boy!* She twisted her mouth dispassionately as she tried to clean her teeth with her tongue.

Thank you for reading my book. Please leave a review of what you thought of my book at your favourite retailer.

Like me on Facebook:
https://www.facebook.com/AGNKayE

Printed in Poland
by Amazon Fulfillment
Poland Sp. z o.o., Wrocław